WITHDRAWN

Jumped In

Jumped In

PATRICK FLORES-SCOTT

DES PLAINES PUBLIC LIBRARY
1501 ELLINWOOD STREET
DES PLAINES, IL 60016

Christy Ottaviano Books

Henry Holt and Company

New York

Henry Holt and Company, LLC
Publishers since 1866
175 Fifth Avenue
New York, New York 10010
macteenbooks.com

Henry Holt® is a registered trademark of Henry Holt and Company, LLC.
Copyright © 2013 by Patrick Flores-Scott.
All rights reserved.

Henry Holt books may be purchased for business or promotional use.
For information on bulk purchases, please contact Macmillan Corporate
and Premium Sales Department at (800) 221-7945 x5442.

Library of Congress Cataloging-in-Publication Data
Flores-Scott, Patrick.
Jumped in / Patrick Flores-Scott. — First edition.
pages   cm
Summary: In the two years since his mother left him with his grand-
parents in Des Moines, Washington, Sam has avoided making friends
and perfected the art of being a slacker, but being paired with a
frightening new student for a slam poetry unit transforms his life.
ISBN 978-0-8050-9514-2 (hardback)—ISBN 978-1-4668-3715-7 (e-book)
[1. Interpersonal relations—Fiction.   2. High schools—Fiction.
3. Schools—Fiction.   4. Poetry—Fiction.   5. Mexican Americans—
Fiction.   6. Family life—Washington (State)—Fiction.   7. Des Moines
(Wash.)—Fiction.]   I. Title.
PZ7.F33435Jum 2013   [Fic]—dc23   2013018844

First Edition—2013 / Designed by Ashley Halsey

Printed in the United States of America by R. R. Donnelley & Sons
Company, Harrisonburg, Virginia

10   9   8   7   6   5   4   3   2   1

For Emma and our boys

HOME

nir·va·na *n def:* an ultimate experience of some pleasurable emotion such as harmony or joy

Nir·va·na *n def:* a legendary kick-ass rock-and-roll band from my hometown of Aberdeen, Washington

I'M THINKING ABOUT RUPE AND DAVE.

My buddies from Aberdeen, out on the Washington coast. It's where I used to live before I was "temporarily" moved away. And it's where Rupe and Dave and I used to dream of becoming the next Nirvana.

The next hard-rocking, ass-kicking, world-famous band from Aberdeen.

A movie rolls in my brain. I'm watching us fish for cutthroat trout from the muddy banks of the Wishkah River. I see Rupert smiling at me with his big ol' buckteeth, his long, rust-red hair flowing in the wind as he baits his hook with a massive, wriggling night crawler. Dave zips back and forth along the bank, a blur of Coke-bottle glasses, dirty blond buzz cut and turbocharged ADHD, pointing and shouting, "Cast here! Cast here, guys!"

We're just little seventh graders fishing and having a good time, but all we can do is argue about Nirvana.

We argue about what Nirvana would be like now if Kurt Cobain hadn't decided to leave this world.

I argue that "Scoff" is a way better song than "Smells Like Teen Spirit," which is awesome, but there's no way it rocks as hard as "Scoff" does.

And Rupe and Dave argue over who should play what when we start our own band.

We wipe the mud and worm and fish muck off our hands and rock-paper-scissors it for who's gonna be Kurt and who's gonna be bassist Krist Novoselic, the two original members of Aberdeen's Nirvana before they added drummer Dave Grohl and became *Seattle's* Nirvana.

We take our *Nirvana Tour of Aberdeen* and walk in the shadows of our idols, sneaking into Aberdeen High School, strutting the halls like we don't give a shit, peeing in the weeds on the banks of the Wishkah, smoking stolen cigarettes beneath the pier at night.

Stalking their ghosts.

Because those guys had something we want.

And we're not gonna stop until we find it.

We hang out at the abandoned old house where Kurt and Krist and a parade of drummers used to rehearse before their band had a name. Dave carves our initials into the peeling white shingles, and we stuff our faces with fat blackberries plucked from the tangle of vines taking over the yard. Sprawled out on the front porch, Rupe writes list after list of possible band names while I scrawl lyrics in my blue spiral notebook and imagine my voice belting those songs out over thumping drums and bass.

We dream of making Aberdeen rock again.

Making the country rock again.

Making the world rock again.

On summer nights, my mom stuffs us full of her incredible barbecue chicken and homemade mac and cheese and s'mores. Lying in the tall grass, under the ancient cedar tree, we press Play on the boom box and lose ourselves in "Scoff," "Paper Cuts," "Swap Meet." We leave our troubles behind, shredding air guitars, pounding imaginary snare drums and tom-toms as we sing like rock stars and float way up to the clouds—then higher and higher, and far, far away, to a whole 'nother world of head-banging nirvana.

That was then.

FLEEING PUGET HIGH SCHOOL

I'M ON A PISSED-OFF WALK IN THE GRAY, DRIZZLING RAIN.

I'm thinking way too much.

I can't stop fucking thinking.

My socks suck up water through worn-out boots. Watching for potholes and mud puddles is nothing but a frustrating waste of time. You're wet if you do, wet if you don't.

It's just the way it is around here.

From Puget High School to my grandparents' house, it's four blocks up Twenty-fourth Street. Eight massive blocks down the steep, never-ending hill on 216th. Every step of the way, the fir trees drip gray and the fat black clouds droop low, dumping buckets of rain into the murky waters of Puget Sound. It cracks me up how people here in Des Moines, and up in Seattle, all love to say that this is one of the most beautiful places in the country. All the evergreen trees and Vashon Island and the Olympic Mountains to the west. Massive, snowcapped Mount Rainier to the southeast. . . .

Beautiful?

Sure.

But who gives a rat's ass if you never get to see any of it? This place is covered in a blanket of gray mush for about nine months a year and it wears on you. It's like the dripping, wet gray takes everything you could see, all the nice stuff, and pulls it out of focus so there's nothing in front of you but fuzz.

Nothing to distract you.

Nothing outside of you to think about.

So you're forced to turn inward, to go deep into the world of your own dark mind.

And that's the last place I wanna go.

So on days like this, I fight to stop the dark thoughts. I struggle to fill my brain with lyrics. I try to think about the most useless crap I can come up with. I think about stupid kids and the stupid things I see them do at school. I think about idiot teachers and the idiotic stuff they say. And I make up lyrics about them.

Lyrics exposing their stupidity.

Lyrics for great songs I'll never write, for cool bands I'll never join.

I spin the loudest Nirvana—the old stuff—the wailing wall of sound stuff, and I fight to leave this place, to float away, to get back to the coast. Back to Aberdeen. Back to Rupe. Back to Dave.

Back to my mom the way she used to be.

But today, the music doesn't come.

I'm stuck solid on the dark, wet, messed-up side of my brain. And it's all the fault of one kid.

Luis Cárdenas.

A THUG IN
NO-MAN'S-LAND

IT HAPPENS IN MS. CASSIDY'S TENTH-GRADE ENGLISH CLASS.

"Scholars to the ready!"

Aw, shit.

It's one of Cassidy's *spring-in-her-step* days.

"I'm sooo excited about this poetry unit, people! Seriously!"

She bounces around talking about metaphor and the senses and the end-of-the-unit poetry slam. "Poetry is meant to be spoken and heard," she says. "So we're going to have to trust each other."

I look around at my "trusted peers," and I know I'm not gonna write a fucking thing for this woman.

"For today's assignment, we're talkin' personification. When might one choose to *personify*?"

Cassidy's voice melts into the never-ending drone of

jumbo jets skimming Puget High School's rooftops. I figure I'm home free for the period, so I pull my hood over my head and tight around my face and lean onto my desk.

Then the door to the class opens and *he* walks through it.

A Mexican gangster with a shaved head and a linebacker's body, he saunters on in and everyone—*everyone*—shifts their focus. All eyes are on this kid.

It's like you can hear the shift. Like you can *feel* it. Like a bunch of tipsy, whale-watching tourists scrambling from one side of the ship deck to the other to catch a glimpse of a breaching orca and they almost tip the boat over.

He's one of *those* types. The type that every girl wants to *do* and every boy wants to *be*. The boys all wanna be him 'cuz the girls all wanna do him. The girls all wanna do him 'cuz he's a bad boy and girls love bad boys. Or maybe it's that he's six feet tall and good-looking.

He hands Cassidy his transfer slip. What does she do?

She looks right at me.

Damn!

It's the seat!

The seat next to mine. *No-Man's-Land.* The empty seat I fight to keep clear in every class. So no one bugs me. No partners. No one to turn and talk to like they're always telling us to do. That empty seat means teachers forget I exist. It means I don't have to act like a fake-ass dumbshit like everybody else. And when the bell rings and class starts, I can lay my head down and disappear under my coat and under my hood and escape from everything.

But right now, that seat is the only empty spot in the whole class.

Cassidy starts walking him my way and they're all looking.

Looking at him.

Looking at *me*.

I feel the glares pelt my skin. My heart thumps hard. The blood rushes to my brain and the red to my face. Cassidy and the kid keep on coming my way and I'm like, *Do not sit there. DO NOT SIT DOWN!* The words ricochet inside my head. I glare at Cassidy with all I got, hoping I can change her mind.

She ignores me and the thug does it. He sits in No-Man's-Land.

"Sam, this is Luis Cárdenas," Ms. Cassidy says fake sweetly.

I don't say hi. I don't say anything to him.

And he doesn't say anything to me.

He just turns away, in slow motion. It's like an action movie where you see a creepy dude for the first time, and you just know he's gonna end up being the bad guy. And he's gonna do something awful to someone before it's over.

He sits there and looks straight ahead without a word.

I look straight ahead too.

To show him I don't care he's there.

We go almost the whole period without even looking at each other.

Until I sneak a quick one.

And I see it.

Holy crap!

He's got the gnarliest, sickest scar on his neck—the side of his neck facing me. Four inches long, just beneath his jawline. It's one of those thick ones that puffs up like a mini mountain range.

I space out and visualize Luis getting his neck slashed in so many ways.

A rival gang member stabs him in a dark back alley.

A bunch of his cholo homies jump him and cut him for his initiation.

He stands in front of the bathroom mirror and coldly does the deed himself because he knows it's gonna make him look like a *badass*.

The pictures keep on coming until ... "What are you looking at?" One mighty vein pops red from his forehead. He clenches his jaw, glaring at me like I'm a complete idiot. Like he's about to kill me.

"Nothin', man." I turn away, trembling.

He huffs and shakes his head.

I see kids tap one another on the shoulder, pointing. Whispers are firing from all directions. Their eyes are accusing me, wondering what I did to him, what I said to him to piss him off. And I know they're all wondering what method Luis is gonna choose to kick my ass.

I plant my head back on my desk and throw my hood over it. I try to block out all the eyes. All the whispers.

I fight hard to breathe.

In.

Out.

I plead with my heart to slow its massive pounding.

In.

Out.

I wait for the blood to flow from my face and make a pact with myself: No staring. No peeks. No glances.

I'm not looking his way ever again.

Poetry Unit: PERSONIFICATION   Name **Luis**
                                    Date / /

Dearest Poets of Room 108,

     We've read and discussed examples of personification in the poems
of Langston Hughes, Maya Angelou, and William Carlos Williams. Soon we'll
discuss examples of personification in *your* poetry. Write about an item from
your daily life. Give that "thing" human characteristics. This will shed light
on both the human experience and the subject of your poem. Deep stuff,
poets. You're deep kids, so I wouldn't have it any other way. Now, make me
proud. Make me weep, laugh, think. . . . Make me happy I went into teaching.
Please! Now get to it!

          Sincerely,

          Ms. Cassidy

Your brilliant ideas:

My Scar: An Old Man in the Community Pool

My scar is old man Pyle
Floating alone in the Highline Pool

The shriveled viejito grandpa
Smiling in his tiny Speedo

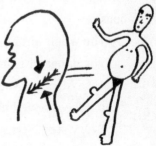

With skin like prune fruit leather
That sags and folds and droops

You stare at Mr. Pyle in his microscopic trunks
Your jaw drops
Your eyebrows scrunch

You don't want to look
     But no matter how hard you try
 You just can't stop looking

—Luis Cárdenas

HE'S EVERYWHERE

THE FINAL BELL IS STILL RINGING AS I BUST THROUGH PUGET'S FRONT DOORS.

The whole situation's exploded.

The gangster is not just in Cassidy's class. He's in all my classes. All six! And the brilliant teachers of Puget High School have seated him in No-Man's-Land in every one.

Every single frickin' one.

STOP NOISE

GRAY SKIES CAVE IN, SHRINKING THE WORLD. The rain pours harder.

I want out of this weather.

I want my bed.

I'm so close I can see Ginny and Bill's house.

But I can't move. I'm stuck boots deep in muddy water, trying to stop his voice. Gilbert's voice. That damn parrot is camped out in my head alongside Luis and the rest of them. And he's screaming it! I'm nowhere near the front door but I hear him louder than ever. I press my hands over my ears, into my brain. I fight to get Krist's bass line from "Scoff" thumping and Kurt's gravel voice surging in . . .

But there is no way.

Gilbert wins.

Gilbert takes me back.

Back to the day my mom's life fell apart. When she lost

her crappy job canning juice at the cranberry plant in Aberdeen. When her idiot boyfriend, Lance, socked her in the jaw and she decided we needed to get away from Aberdeen and head to Grandma Ginny and Grandpa Bill's.

It was just after school let out after seventh grade. I had plans to go salmon fishing with Rupe and his dad. Dave had gotten a real electric guitar from his uncle and Rupe's grandma had bought him an old beat-up drum set. We were shopping for a used bass for me. This high school kid was selling what he claimed was the very first bass Krist Novoselic ever played. Who knows if it was true or bullshit? The point is we were finally growing our hair out. Finally kick-starting our band.

I picture myself reassuring Rupe and Dave that we'll be up and rocking as soon as I get back in a couple weeks. I tell them my mom needs this little break. I tell them she deserves it after what she's been through lately.

I grab some clothes and my blue lyrics notebook. My mom and I hop in the car and set out east on the Olympic Highway.

In the afternoon we get to Ginny and Bill's little Des Moines rambler. We walk in the door and there's a birdcage right there. Ginny introduces us to her new pet, Gilbert. She says he's an African Grey parrot and she calls him my cousin. She tells us he talks, but he's shy.

They feed us ham sandwiches and potato salad for lunch. Bill—all gussied up in his flannel shirt, bolo tie, and cowboy boots—motions for me to join him for a Fudgsicle in the living room. He shows off a model of the Boeing 737 jet he and Ginny used to build before they retired from the factory. He shows me snapshots from his hunting days, laughing from the gut about the time he and his buddy Anderson got treed by an elk.

From the kitchen, Ginny yells, "Don't believe a word that old man says, Sam." We all laugh and I figure these couple weeks won't be so bad.

He goes on with the stories and when he finally takes a breath, I hear Ginny—perky positive Grandma Ginny—turn serious in the kitchen, asking my mom all these questions like *How long do you think you'll be, Anne? Do you have friends there? Wait, who is that again? Do you have a job? Money?*

This whole thing is sounding like a big deal. So I head in there to see what's going on and my mom is like, *I have to. I need sun. I have to go.*

The words are a massive kick in the gut.

How long are we going for, Mom?

She grabs me by the shoulders and looks at me with a plastered-on smile. She says she has to leave me here in Des Moines for a short stay. She's heading for Phoenix, Arizona, to see an old friend from high school and get her head on straight. Then she'll come get me and we'll go back to Aberdeen and start over.

Start over? Who needs to start over?

My mom is talking so fast she can't catch her breath. Her face turns pinker than the walls. She's got her fingers locked on my arms. I look at my mom's hands and they're beet red, but the ends of her fingers are bone white. She starts sobbing, going on and on about how sorry she is, saying all this trash about my loser dad—who's never been there to defend himself—and hugging me and freaking out that I won't hug her back.

I can't be in the same room with her, so I break out of her squeeze and barricade myself in the bathroom. No matter how much she begs and screams, I won't come out.

I focus on the green wallpaper with the repeating pheasant-and-duck pattern. The birds are flying around some sunny mountain lake. I would do anything to be there with them.

I want my mom to go.

I close my eyes and wish her away.

Her bawling gets even louder and more intense. She pounds the door with a slow *bam-bam-bam*—and through her sobbing, slobbering tears, she screams, "GOOD-BYE, SAM!" I mean, my mom *screams* it. And she sprays all her fear and anger and hurt all at once.

All at me.

It was the first time I can remember my heart pounding like it does now—like a jackhammer—and my face stinging like it's a pincushion for pissed-off bees.

I wish I could forget.

I *could* have.

I think I would have.

If it wasn't for fucking Gilbert!

From his living room perch, he saw it all. Heard everything and recorded the moment in his pea brain. Locked it in forever.

So ever since that horrible day, whether I'm coming or going, I can't get past Gilbert's cage without him screeching, "GOOD-BYE, SAM! GOOD-BYE, SAM! GOOD-BYE, SAM!" I hear my mom's trembling voice and see her crying eyes. And I feel just like I did that afternoon two years ago.

Every day this happens.

Every day I'm transported back.

Every day, at least twice a day, the stupid bird does this to me.

Everyone experiences a painful moment in life. But not everyone has to relive the moment every . . . single . . . day.

I do.

Thanks to a stupid parrot.

I feel the rain pelt my face as I sprint toward the house. Past the mailbox. Up the gravel driveway. Through the muddy yard.

I bust through the front door and I'm met with the screech: "GOOD-BYE, SAM!"

I jump at his cage.

"GOOD-BYE, SAM! GOOD-BYE, SAM!"

I wrestle with the latch until the door pops open.

I reach in and Gilbert pecks my hand. Claws my fingers. I clutch his scrawny neck and lift him out of there. I squeeze. He tries to wiggle free. I squeeze his neck harder. I swear he's looking into me, pleading for his pathetic little life.

I see horror in his eyes.

I see me reflected in them.

What in the hell, Sam?

What are you doing?

I let go of his little neck and he immediately inflates. "GOOD-BYE, SAM! GOOD-BYE, SAM!" He screeches it louder than ever.

I push him back in his cage.

"GOOD-BYE, SAM! GOOD-BYE, SAM!"

I latch the door and haul ass into my room.

"GOOD-BYE, SAM! GOOD-BYE, SAM!"

He's always gonna say it.

And there's nothing I can do about it.

I collapse on the bed, pull the covers over my head and try to check out.

But I can't lose the images.

Gilbert's eyes.

The look on Luis's face.

The look on those idiot kids' faces.

My mom's face, eyes, fingers . . . the sound of her scream . . .

Stop thinking, Sam!

Stop.

Just press Play.

I run my fingers over the player till I hit the button.

Do-do, dow-ow, do-do dow-ow. It's "Big Long Now."

The distorted guitar is a slow steady hop. A cymbal rolls. Kick drum and toms. Krist's bass loops up and down, somehow pushing the rhythm while holding it back. The most haunted voice ever seeps into the noise, then soars above it all.

I fight to feel Kurt's pain. Fight to forget about mine.

I watch a thousand raindrops run down my window. Watch mold grow on the sill. Watch darkness come. "Big Long Now" plays over and over, and all I can think is how this music used to make me want to be something good.

Now I just want it to take me away.

What the hell happened, Sam?

QUIET IN MY MIND

The noise finally stops
    When I'm with you again.

I feel you here in my room
      One more time
Your great big hand on my shoulder
Your dark eyes locked on mine
     As you tuck me in with your best stories.

Stories about my ox-strong grandpapi, Victor
About the good old days in Mexicali
About the lime trees lining Hidalgo Street
    Where you ran wild as a kid.

Lights out with a kiss on my forehead

I say, Good night, Papi

You say, Good night, mijo
    I'll stay here till you're snoring good
      Don't worry, mijo
        I'll stay right here.

—Luis Cárdenas

THE RULES

"Sammy, if you walk, you're going to be late." It's Ginny. She's knocking on my door. "Get yourself dressed and hop in the car. No need to thank me."

I had no intention of going back to school today. No intention of seeing Luis. It's what I get for pressing the snooze too many times.

Ginny drives and chats while I try to hold my shit together.

This year was shaping up perfect; I was anonymous in school. I was forgotten. I was alone. Now I got Luis and classes full of staring kids.

I reassure myself I can make it all go away.

I've done it before. I'll do it again.

I'll burrow deeper than ever, until nobody knows I even exist. Until I disappear again.

I can do this. Because I've got a plan. I've got strategies that have worked for two whole years. I've got ... *the Rules*:

1. Don't be late to class.
2. Don't screw around.
3. Don't ever look the teacher in the eye.
4. Don't ever look a classmate in the eye.
5. Develop your blank stare.

Work on it. Practice it. Use it. The blank stare is your best friend.

6. Don't ever raise your hand.

No matter how well you know the answer or how much you wanna correct your classmates' stupid-ass comments, if you raise your hand and show how smart you are, the teacher will be all over you. They love the intelligent ones. They'll get to know your name and it's all over. Kiss anonymity good-bye. So don't ever, ever raise your hand.

Number 7 is the tricky one. A lot of slackers totally screw up number 7.

7. Listen.

That's right. *Listen* to everything.

Regardless of how hard you try to disappear, every once in a blue moon, the teacher will lob a question your way. The worst thing you can do is act clueless. *Cluelessness* means you're not listening, and that means you got a lecture coming. And the very last thing you want is a lecture. A lecture is the first step to a teacher deciding he wants to be on your case.

Say the teacher asks you a direct question, making attention unavoidable. What should you do? You should answer correctly. You can do that because you've been listening. You've avoided the attention that comes with a lecture.

Good.

Now the new problem is that your teacher thinks he's got you because you were listening and you know the answer. He thinks you're hooked into his lesson. He thinks you might even be smart. Now he's gonna come at you with the follow-up question quicker than you can duck.

The *follow-up question* is the time for *cluelessness*.

No matter how smart you think you are, no matter if you've got the right answer or an interesting opinion, be strong—follow my advice and hold your tongue. Slowly shake your head, shrug your shoulders, and flash your perfected slow . . . blank . . . stare. Hang in there with the stare and your teacher will give up. He'll be satisfied that you were listening, but reassured that you're not the sharpest cheddar on the platter and you're not worth spending a lot of extra time on. He'll move on to harass the next poor sap, and you're good for a couple weeks.

At least.

Especially if you're following rules 1 through 6.

There are two kinds of slackers. First, there are those idiots who love attention and are willing to engage their teachers and classmates, and get into all kinds of trouble.

Then there are those who just wanna be invisible. Being the first kind is easy. Being the invisible kind is *not* easy. You have to seriously want it to make it happen. But desire is not enough. You must reach a level of self-discipline that rivals only the most successful, suck-up, straight-A scholars.

I've got the desire. I've got the discipline.

And I've got a system that works.

OJOS MEANS "EYES" MEANS "YOU BETTER WATCH IT"

I PULL OPEN PUGET'S FRONT DOOR, and just like every other morning, I'm jolted by the screeches and squeals from Viking cheerleaders. Eyes to the ground, I squeeze past them and their rich, waterfront, Briar Park friends as they compare iPhone apps and ski trips and remind me that I hate this place.

I make my way into B Hall, pushing through the jocks and goths and losers—the Des Moines Hill kids who are supposed to be my people.

Then it's out to the covered corridor and through C Hall and the poor kids who live on and around Pacific Highway.

Between here and Cassidy's, I gotta pass through Cholo Corner. It's where all the Latino boys from Mr. Bell's English Language Learner class hang out. They all practice looking tough and never say anything to anyone except their badass friends.

I scan the place for Luis, but I don't see him anywhere.

I pull both hood strings tight and keep moving with my eyes on the floorboards, then—

BAM!

I smack right into one of those kids.

"*Ojos,* man." He reaches a hand up and pulls my hood back. He gets in my face and says, "You better watch yourself."

Shit. It's Carlos Díaz, notorious fuck-up cholo.

"Sorry."

"Not a thing, man. I ain't got no beef with you. But Luis does. Yeah, *Callado* wants to kick your ass."

I knew it.

"That's the word, man. Everybody sayin'."

Everybody?

"They all talkin'. Saying you been starin' Luis down and he wanna mess you up. And no disrespect, but I wouldn't mind watchin' that shit go down. What class you got?"

I pace forward and back as my skin catches fire. My heart pounds like Krist Novoselic's bass on "Paper Cuts" as I picture Luis tearing me apart.

I take off toward the main building.

But I don't get anywhere because Carlos—who's a head shorter than me and a ton stronger—has a vise grip on my arm.

"You can't be a pussy," he says. "It'll make everything worse. Now, I'm pretty sure I asked you what class you got."

"Cassidy."

"I'm coming with you."

As we walk, I feel another me float out of my body. I hover

above myself watching the second scariest kid in school haul me to get my ass kicked by the first.

Outside Cassidy's room, Carlos lets go of my shaking arm and grabs my face. Slaps my cheek a couple times and says, "Relax yourself, kid. Relax your mind. You wanna be loose doin' battle. Now, if I was you, I'd start with your left. Quick jabs. Keep your feet moving. And mitts up! Even if it ain't much to look at, you gotta protect that mug. Jab left, punch right. Got it?"

I've got no reply. So Carlos says, "Forget all that shit I just said. Just stand there and jellyfish your body and it'll be over real quick. And don't worry, I'll be right out here watching the whole thing."

I head into class, and everyone turns around to see what's gonna happen. They all watch me sit my butt down by Luis.

My head gets tingly and my guts turn over. I put my head on my desk, and when I do, I notice that not *everyone* is looking at me.

Luis isn't.

He's just sitting there like the ass-kicking thug he is.

I force myself to sit up.

Luis acts like I'm not even there.

Cassidy pushes her accountant glasses up her nose as she rises from her messy desk. She pulls her frizzy black hair into a bunch, grabs a rubber band from between her teeth and ties the whole tangle into a bouncing pouf.

"All right, class. All right. Settle yourselves." She claps her hands a couple times. "It's pop-poetry time so just knock one out. Don't think too much. Just jot it down. Describe a flower. Wrap it in a metaphor. *Bam!* You got a poem! Nothing to it. Personify your seat partner's nose. *Boo-ya!* Poem! Just free your mind and let that little sucker flow into your journal. This is going to be a daily ritual throughout the entirety of the unit, so get used to it, people."

Forget her, Sam.

Just look straight ahead.

Pretend he's not even there.

Focus on the Rules.

And breathe. Just breathe.

I try all that. But I'm distracted by annoying tapping.

It's Luis. He's got his fingernails going manic on the desk.

Cassidy starts walking our way. He sees her and says it real fast. Straight ahead, like he's talking to the whiteboard in front of class. "You got a pencil?"

I'm not sure I heard right. But if I did, he could only be talking to me.

"Pencil. You got a pencil?"

A pencil, a pencil, a pencil ... I pat my coat pockets like there might be a pencil there, but it's ridiculous because I never bring one to class. I take in a deep, slow breath. I feel like I'm gonna faint. I look down at my feet and it's my lucky day because there's an eraserless, chewed-up pencil right under the table. I pick it up and pass it to Luis.

He gives me a half grunt and nods straight ahead in thanks, I think. Then he curls over his journal and pretends to write.

The class gets to popping out poems.

For the moment, all is well.

Then straight-A geek Julisa Mendez—on her way back from chatting up Cassidy—walks past us, stops and looks at Luis like she can't believe what she just saw.

Luis looks up from his fake-scribbling right back at her.

And—*whoosh!*—every eye is on us.

Julisa walks up to him and pulls his pencil out of his hand. Holds it up for inspection. "Seriously, Luis? This is disgusting."

There are snickers from the class.

Go away, Julisa!

She walks over and tosses the pencil in the trash.

Do not come back here.

Do not—

She comes back all right, and she's got her bulging, orange and green, flower-covered pencil pouch with her.

The eyes all follow her every move.

My heart pounds.

I slump down in my seat as Julisa stands there digging in the ridiculous pouch. She eyes the class and says, "What are you all looking at?" as she pulls out a newly sharpened, perfect blue pencil and slaps it on Luis's desk. Then she looks over at my empty hands and shakes her head.

I pop my hood on and slump harder as she thrusts her hand back into the pouch. "I don't know which is worse," she says. And she slaps a shiny yellow one down for me. "Guys, I'm here every day. Just ask."

Luis doesn't say a word.

I don't say a word.

We just stare straight ahead.

MY FAULT

THE BELL RINGS. I'm the first one out.

But there's no escape. Carlos is right there.

"What happened?" he asks.

"Nothing."

"Aw, shit. Serious?" He looks 100 percent disappointed Luis didn't destroy me. Then he brightens up and says, "Oh, I get it. *Callado* making you sweat this thing out first. That's just like him. What class you got next?"

Vice Principal Carter appears out of nowhere and says, "Mr. Díaz, I have something awesome I want you to see!" He scratches his head. "I forget what it's called. Oh, yeah! It's called your second-period class. You're going to love it."

"You ever try comedy, Mr. C.?"

"Every day, Carlos."

They take a few steps toward Mr. Bell's class, then Carter

turns around and says to me, "Samuel Gregory, how 'bout a smile today? This place isn't all that bad."

Dude's a dope.

Then Carlos shouts, "*Ojos, guëy!* Keep your eyes open!"

"That's enough, Mr. Díaz," Carter says, hauling him away.

I take my seat in Mr. McClean's geometry class.

Check my left. My right.

All I see is kids sinking into their pre-math stupor. Pretending they're doing McClean's problem of the day. Screwing around. Flirting. Texting under their desks.

Not one of them is looking at me. Nobody thinks I'm gonna get my ass kicked in math today. I take in a deep breath and tell myself, *Just follow the Rules, Sam. Just follow the Rules. It's gonna be fine.*

Then Luis walks in.

Thirty pairs of eyes lock on his every step.

He sits down next to me.

And thirty pairs of eyes lock on *us.*

Luis looks my way for a split second. I look away. Scan the class. I'm not imagining a thing. Everyone is checking me out.

Sixty eyes times six classes a day times five days a week times . . .

This is the way it is.

All thanks to him.

I pound my thigh with my fist because it's not true.

This is my fault too.

For talking too much back then.

I drift away from this desk and this 'hood and McClean's

sophomore geometry class. I'm back in front of ancient Ms. Ames's eighth-grade homeroom at Rainier Middle School the fall after my mom dropped me off.

Ms. Ames introduces me as the new kid.

"I won't be here for long," I tell the class. "This is a short-term deal."

Days roll by.

I keep telling kids that it won't be much longer.

"My mom's on her way to get me."

I repeat this out loud, over and over.

"I'll be moving back to Aberdeen real soon."

And I believe it.

So I don't try to make friends.

I don't want new friends.

I don't wanna have anything to do with these Des Moines eighth graders who are ignorant and have never even heard of the Melvins or Mudhoney, or Tad, which I can't even believe.

When kids try to talk to me, I tell them my mom is on a big tour with her rock band and I'll be heading back home in a couple months, even though by now it's clear to everybody this line is complete bullshit.

But I stick to the story because I don't know what else to do.

I tell made-up tales about what far-off city she's in now (LA, Boston, Amsterdam, Moscow—the cities keep on getting farther and farther away), and I make up the name of her all-woman band: Superflame (*wtf?*).

When they ask, I tell them my mom is an amazing drummer. When they don't ask, I tell them the Superflame bassist used to be in Hole and the lead guitar player is from Sleater-Kinney, which means nothing to these kids because they don't know a damn thing about their own Northwest rock-'n'-roll history.

So they start teasing me.

Always asking me when I'll be leaving town. Wondering aloud what I'm wondering silently—if my mom forgot about me.

I keep to myself.

I stop with the stories.

But it doesn't help. I become *the kid who's moving back to Aberdeen to become a rock star, so don't bother getting to know him.* And *the kid whose mom ran off and joined the circus or something.*

They make crack after crack about it. I'm the center-of-attention joke for months. And it's my own damn fault for talking too much.

So I withdraw even farther. And I pray for my mom to come back.

She doesn't.

I pull away from everyone, and after a while, I pretty much quit talking altogether.

It's been two years. I'm a *sophomore.* I shouldn't still be stuck like this. But the pit I've dug for myself feels so deep, I can't climb out of it.

I want to.

I want to climb out and join the world.

But I can't.

I don't know how.

FIRE!

BAM-BAM-BAM!

It's the middle of the night and there's pounding on my door.

"Fire, Sam!" It's Bill. "There's a fire, boy!"

I bolt up. Can't see a thing.

I'm frantic. Scrambling. Running into walls.

Banging my way into the door.

Somehow locating the knob.

Twisting it.

Flinging the door open.

"Hi, Sam."

It's Ginny. She's standing there in her apron, working some pizza dough in her hands. Bill's eating a Fudgsicle.

"Son, we need to talk to you about something," Bill says.

"Isn't there a—"

"No fire. You're just really hard to wake up."

Seriously?

Ginny gets all smiley and excited and sings, "Sam-u-el! There's a very special day-ay, coming soo-oon! In just a few wee-eeks. . . ." She whistles "Happy Birthday to You." "This is a special one. You're turning sixteen! Sixteen years old! Can you imagine?"

"I guess."

"Close your eyes, Sam, and just imagine it." She closes her eyes. "Oh, to be sixteen—"

"All right, Gin," Bill says, looking at her like she's flat nuts. "Sam, we want to make this birthday a great one. Anything you'd like, you name it. Laser tag. Space Needle. Fishing trip. Whatever. It's up to you."

"Okay."

We stand there and it's clear they're waiting for me to say something. So I ask what time it is.

"Six thirty. *Dinnertime*," Ginny sings. "We're having Chinese pizza!"

"No thanks. I'm really tired."

"But, Samuel—"

"Ginny, let's give the boy some peace. Night, Sam." They retreat into their part of the house.

I flop back on my mattress and stare up toward the sky.

A movie of me and Rupe and Dave projects onto the ceiling.

We're all standing around a Chinook salmon piñata hung from the cedar tree in the massive backyard of our Aberdeen rental.

Rupe's got the blindfold on. He's flailing around with the stick, missing the piñata repeatedly, whiffing and hyperventilating, while Dave rolls on the ground, laughing his ass off. I'm laughing my ass off too, as my mom snaps shots in the background with her old Polaroid camera.

She's smiling. She looks really happy.

All of us do.

The brain movie fades to white, and I can't help thinking maybe I made all this happiness stuff up.

I go to my closet, reach deep into the moldy, musty darkness. I grab the backpack I brought from Aberdeen when Bill and Ginny hauled me out there to get some clothes and stuff after they realized I'd probably be staying with them for a while.

I unzip it and root around, hoping the photos are in there.

They are.

There's a hilarious shot of Rupe and Dave shoving cake in my face and one of me with my mom. I'm showing off the Soundgarden poster she gave me and she's holding a home-made German chocolate cake with twelve candles. I'm looking up at her big brown eyes. Her freckles. Long brown hair. The look on my face says I must have the coolest mom in the world.

I take the picture to the bathroom and look in the mirror.

I've got her eyes. A few of her dark brown freckles. Got zits I didn't have then. We all have a summer's worth of tan in those pictures. I feel like I've been pasty pale ever since.

My pudgy face is all stretched and long now. Skinny. Bony. Too bony. Makes me look even more like her. But the pudgy face I had in that photo . . . it was smiling. We all were. We were happy. We had a great time out there in Aberdeen.

Back in my room, I shove the photos in the pack and think about Ginny and Bill.

And I wonder if there's a nice way to tell them to stop bugging me about my birthday.

I turn the light out and swat the box. Kurt sings me away.

I'M SO DEAD

In class, Cassidy's reciting ridiculous poetry.

It's been a week since Luis moved in. He hasn't beaten me up, and it doesn't look like he's going to. Hasn't said a word to me. I haven't even looked at him. I've followed the Rules and the kids seem bored with us now. Hardly any staring at all.

"'*In a summer season when soft was the sun*'—hear all those *esses*, people? Yeah?" Cassidy tilts her head toward her shoulder and her frizzy hair pouf bounces from side to side. "THAT is a beautiful little device used by poets. And what do we call it? Dear scholars, I thank you for asking." She strolls between desks, a smug smirk pasted on her face and a twinkle in her eye. "We call it . . . *alliteration!*" She howls it as she walks past Luis and me like we're not even there.

It's the same with Mrs. Nguyen and Mr. McClean and the rest of them. It never fails. The new kid in class always gets a grace period. Even if it's just a schedule change, like Luis. The teacher will ignore the kid, let him chill for a few days before she starts tightening the screws and getting on his case with the questions and the *Where's your homework?* and the rest of the crap.

It's all right for now. But when Luis's grace period is over? And teachers start coming after him?

They're gonna notice the hooded lug sitting next to him.

And they're gonna come after me.

"Even rap artists use alliteration," Cassidy says. "Let's see here." She takes a quick sip of water from her mug and dramatically clears her throat. "And two, three, four!" she shouts, cupping a hand to her mouth, beat boxing, then knocking out a bordering-on-offensive imitation of a rapper: *"Let me slip you this tip/Don't risk it/If you rip lines and trip/ keep yo' bizness tight-lipped."*

My.

God.

"Thank you!" she barks.

Some suck-up claps.

"Thank you all, my adoring fans. That *assonance*—repetition of vowel sounds—is brought to you by the brilliant hip-hop artist Percy, people! Wait a second: Hi*p*-ho*p*? *P*ercy? *P*eople?" she says, popping her *p*'s. "*Consonance*, anyone? Goodness gracious, golly, guys—Oh, no, you *di-int* alliterate again! Soon this situation must call for a student to stand up and stop this silliness before someone succumbs to the insanity! Seriously."

Cassidy laughs at her hilarious joke as she takes a gulp from her mug. "Scholars, check out 'The Death of the Hired Man' on the second page of today's handout. It's by Robert Frost, who happens to rock my world."

She takes a step toward Luis and me.

Shit! What is she doing?

She flashes an evil grin and teases, "Let's see here . . ."

She's coming right at us.

I'm having an anxiety attack as she ponders whom she'll torture.

"Mr. Cárdenas!"

All eyes on the gangster!

"Let's see if you've been listening."

Grace period over. It's the beginning of the end for me, I just know it.

"Luis, what is the term we use to describe a poet's repeated use of a sound in a line of verse?"

"Uh," he grunts. Some smartass chuckles. Cassidy throws the kid a dirty look. I shrink in my seat thinking Luis doesn't have a clue. *Cluelessness means you got a lecture coming.*

"It's alliteration," Luis says.

Holy crap, he was listening!

"You are correct, sir!" Cassidy hollers.

A collective "whoa" fills the room.

"Well done, Mr. Cárdenas." She's beaming. It's clear she's excited that Luis might actually have a brain and her dream of being the teacher from *Freedom Writers*—her favorite movie—may finally come true.

"Can you give us an example from the first stanza of 'The Death of the Hired Man'?"

It's the *effing follow-up question*! And it's so easy an idiot could get it right. Luis is clearly no idiot. He's gonna know the answer, and the questions from Cassidy are gonna come flying our way fast and furious from now on.

He tilts his head back.

This is it. It's coming.

Cassidy waits for the answer.

But Luis isn't giving her anything.

He's looking in the lights, like he's searching for the answer up there.

What the hell?

He's taking forever. Inside I'm thinking, *It's obvious! It's "Mary sat musing" and "Waiting for Warren"! It's right there on the page, you dumbass!*

Everyone's looking.

My heart's pounding. My face is a tomato.

They're whispering.

What are they saying?

Luis takes in a deep breath and doesn't let it go. He holds the air in one cheek for a while, then bounces it back and forth from one to the other a few times. Finally, he lets the air out in a long, slow, steady stream.

Come on!

My heart's trying to blast its way out of my chest. My head is scorching, stinging as the whispers shoot past me like machine gun bullets.

I want it to be over.

I just want it all to stop.

I want Cassidy to go away.

I want the stares to go away.

Just then, a kid comes into class with a note.

"Hold on a sec," she tells Luis, holding a finger in the air. She examines the note and starts talking to the kid.

It's my only chance.

So I take it.

I do the worst thing ever.

I talk to Luis.

I whisper him the answer.

"It's 'Mary sat musing' and 'Waiting for Warren'!"

You idiot, Sam!

You dumbass!

What are you thinking?

You broke your own goddamn Rules!

I look straight ahead. *Did he hear me?*

I look at the floor. *Did Cassidy? Did anyone hear me?*

I breathe in.

Out.

I wanna die right here.

Right now.

I've got the image of Luis's angry eyes glaring at me when he caught me staring at his scar. Somehow, I know this is worse.

"Well, Mr. Cárdenas, what have you got for us?"

Luis is not saying anything.

Cassidy hovers. Looks concerned.

Folds her arms.

Unfolds them.

Loses her smile.

Finds it again.

My God, this is taking forever!

I sneak a peek at him.

And can't believe what I see.

Luis's face goes plastic—no expression at all—as he slowly shakes his head back and forth at Cassidy.

Then back and forth some more, even slower.

No.

Freaking.

Way.

He's shooting her the *blank stare*!

"Earth to Luis . . . you in there?" Cassidy pleads.

He just gives her more of the stare.

"You told me what alliteration is, so read the first stanza again and find the example."

He just shakes his head *no,* like he's an idiot. I gotta respect him because he's taking a strong stand. He's not gonna let Cassidy know that he knows.

She looks completely crushed.

Then she smiles the way teachers smile when they quit on you. When there's no hope.

And she moves on. "All right, class. Who can help us out?"

Then it hits me: He's never late. Never talks back. No eye contact. Never raises his hand. Now he's been caught listening *and* thinking . . . and evading the follow-up with a classically executed *blank stare*!

Luis is following the Rules.

ONE THING IN COMMON

IS HE COPYING ME?

Did he come up with the Rules on his own?

It doesn't matter. I breathe in and let it out, relieved, because maybe, just maybe, that was it for the questions from Cassidy.

Because both of us are following the Rules.

Maybe everything's gonna be okay.

Maybe my life can go back to normal.

Just as I think it, Luis leans over to me and says, "Do that again, and I swear I'll kill you."

I WON'T DO THAT AGAIN

WOULD I HAVE BEEN ANGRY if Luis had so blatantly broken a Rule and threatened my peace?

Yes, I would have.

Would I have felt like killing him?

Yes, I would have.

Would I have killed him?

No, I wouldn't have killed him.

Kids say "I'm gonna kill you" all the time. But when they say "kill," they don't really mean *kill*.

But Luis isn't just a kid.

He's a gangster.

And what do gangsters do? Besides tag buildings, steal cars and guns, and deal drugs?

They kill people.

And that fucking scares me.

On the other hand, if Luis is such a badass, why would he work so hard to follow the Rules? To try to *not* be noticed? To try and disappear?

Like I do?

Why is it important to him? What makes him that way? Why would he care? He's a big, cold-blooded, cholo gangster with a scary neck scar.

A cold-blooded cholo who just threatened to kill my ass.

Stuck, Waiting

Papi, I'm stuck somewhere between you and me

And here in the middle
    Is a big bunch of nada ... nothing ... zero

On one side it's you, Papi
    And your legacy of machismo
And Rubén telling me I've got to follow you
    It's hard not to ...

On the other side are my crazy dreams
    What I want to do
You've heard that saying:
    "To your own self be true"

I want to be who I want to be
    But vatos are pressing me
Making sure this apple doesn't roll
    Too far from the tree

So I'm stuck in the middle
    Where I've been since I was little
Succeeding at posing like a wannabe
    Failing in school
        Hiding what's inside of me

Papi, if you were still here
    Would you set me free?
        Let me be me?

Please give me a sign
    Tell me it's okay
That I don't have to
    Live and die your way

That I can be my own man
    Free
Cut loose from your past
    To create my own legacy

Give me a sign
    I'll be all right in the meantime
Here in the middle
        Missing you
           Watching for you
             Listening for you
               Waiting...

—Luis Cárdenas

TELL US ALL ABOUT *THE LIFE,* GANGSTER BOY

It's a couple days after the incident. Luis and I sit in Cassidy's class, eyes trained on the board, following rules 3 and 4.

We're ready for anything Cassidy might dish out as she starts in on *metaphors*. We both follow rule 7.

She asks for "an example of a metaphor for our society." We follow rule 6.

Smartass Mick Weatherspoon does not follow rule 6. He fires his hand up and Cassidy calls on him. He asks if gangs could be a metaphor for society.

Possibly a deep question.

But at the moment, I can't give a rat's ass because Cassidy's knee jerks and she immediately turns to get feedback from Luis. Like he's the class expert. Like he's dying to educate us all about gangbanger life.

She walks right at us.

I can't believe she's coming back at him so soon after he blank-stared her down.

I freak out about all the looks from the class. But I'm not worried about Luis. He's gonna prevail again.

Cassidy's standing directly over him and she says, "Luis, what's your take on—"

It's all she can get out.

She's frozen.

Stuck in her tracks.

Luis hasn't done anything. Hasn't said a word. But Cassidy is stopped cold.

You can see the wheels turning in her head. She's looking up at the ceiling, thinking the whole thing through.

It's quiet.

The furnace clanks in the corner.

A jumbo jet slowly whooshes overhead.

Cassidy looks down at the ground. She turns and walks away from Luis. And she completely changes the subject.

It's awkward. But for the moment, the attention isn't on Luis. It's on Cassidy. Everyone is checking her out, wondering what the hell made her stop like that.

The bell rings and the class bolts up to go.

Cassidy's off the hook.

But she doesn't take the free pass.

As Luis walks toward the door, she stops him. "Luis, I hope you don't think that I've assumed anything about you. Because I haven't."

He doesn't respond. He just stands there for a long time.

Then he looks up at her like he wants to say something, but he can't. He struggles to talk, but no words come out.

Carlos called Luis *Callado*. I looked it up. It means quiet, or like, the Quiet One. Well, *Callado* is all he is until he dashes out of the classroom.

Running.

Without a word.

CALLADO

I'm *Callado*

Still waters, aguas quietas

But in school you have to speak
To be seen as running deep

To be thought of as more than
The tragic mask
I wear to put you off
I don't know why, so don't ask

Someday I'll scrap the mask
I'll let loose my new, crazy words
I'll speak my piece
Without ceasing till you've learned...

That I'm as deep
As Everest is voluminous

I'm as thoughtful
As the sun is luminous

As lucid
As Casanova is amorous

As passionate
As a grizzly is carnivorous

And as curious
As the universe is enormous.

But until then
Will you take
My rhyming words for it?
Because I don't yet
Know how to say it
Can't convey it
So I want you to assume it:
That just because I'm quiet
Doesn't mean I don't
Have a lot to say.

(Please keep on asking me
I know I'll get it out right someday.)

—Luis Cárdenas

ON A STRING

ON MY WAY TO CLASS, I'm trying to figure out what made Luis run from Cassidy.

And just like that I smack into—

"*Ojos,* man. You never *not* bumping me?"

Aw, hell.

"You gotta keep your head up, son!"

"I'm just going to class, so—"

"*Callado* beat the shit outta you yet?"

"Nah—"

"Serious?"

"No—I mean, yes, I'm serious."

I try to take off, but Carlos pulls me back to him. He looks to make sure no one's listening and says, "Ain't no *vato* in this pen don't fear *Callado*." Carlos pinches his thumb and finger right in front of my eyes. "He's got us all right here," he says, "on a motherfuckin' string."

"Uh-huh."

"So whattaya gotta do?"

"I . . . um . . . I–"

"Don't you listen to nothing I say?"

"I do. I listen."

"You gotta keep your eyes open."

"That's what I was gonna say."

"Do it, then."

I nod my head, noting that I'm being singled out by a kid who missed half of last year when Mel, the security guard, got tipped that he had a knife in his locker and was gonna jump this junior, Marcus Shelton. Mr. Carter and Mel went into Carlos's locker and found the knife and a bunch of weed and figured out Carlos had been dealing at school. That same day, the cops busted some older gangbanger friends of Carlos's who were sneaking onto campus to help him beat the shit out of Marcus.

So, if Carlos is that much of a badass and *he's* afraid of Luis, how bad must Luis be?

"He ever say anything to you?"

I shake my head.

"Nothin'?"

I shake my head again.

"Well, if he ever say anything about me, or about his crazy brother Rubén—they call him Flaco. Flaco-Rubén. Rubén-Flaco. Same dude—or he say anything about Flaco's crew, Sixteenth Street—you gotta tell me what the fuck is up.

'Cuz Luis and me . . . we're not talkin' much lately. It's not a beef or nothin'. It's more like he's on his own trip and I don't wanna piss his angry ass off. So if you hear anything, you lemme know what he says. We straight?" Carlos offers me his fist. So I pound him, knuckles to knuckles. "That's my boy," he says.

I run my ass inside and take my seat by Luis. He's on time, looking stone cold as usual.

The bell rings, and Cassidy starts flippin' shit about poetry.

I think about what Carlos asked me to do.

Well, you can forget about that, because I'm not telling anyone anything. Even if I *do* hear something, I'm keeping my mouth shut.

DYING TO KNOW

Carlos
I'm onto you
And your
Parasite wannabes
Following me
With owl eyes
And rubber necks
Nodding
When our paths cross
Like you're
My longtime homie

Pretending you know me
'Cuz of the way I dress
And who my brother is
And who your cousin is
And who my papi was

Carlos
I know why you're
Putting on this show
It's all because
You're dying to know

Dying to know about
What I've seen
Where I've been
And how it all went down
When I got jumped in
About my badass papi

And how he rose to the top
And all the shit about my brother
Who's even badder than my pop

Carlos
You're dying to know
Going crazy to know
Facts
Details
Descriptions
Gossip
Dirt
You're dying to know
Dying to know

Carlos
Here's a piece of information
If you still haven't heard
I'm never going to talk to you
Not one single word
So set yourself free
Or die waiting
Die waiting for me

Carlos
If you die
Dying to know
That would be the saddest
Most pathetic way to go

Dying
Dying to know ...

Carlos
Don't die
Dying to know

Don't die
Dying to know

DON'T DIE
DYING TO KNOW

—Luis Cárdenas

LUIS AND THE GO-TO GIRL

It's the third week of the unit–the third week of Luis–and we've made it to rough-draft poetry sharing day.

"I am so excited to hear from my brilliant poets!" Cassidy hollers. "This is going to be awesome."

Awesome? You can't use the word *awesome* by itself to describe rough-draft poetry sharing day. Nope, for *awesome* to work in this context, you'd have to team it up with some other words, like *amount of steaming bullshit.*

"I need a volunteer to start things off."

That can only mean one awesome thing.

It means Julisa Mendez takes her hand out of her pencil pouch and shoots it in the air, volunteering to go first, as always. And it means, as always, my gag reflex sets in.

"Listen for her use of imagery," Cassidy begs after Julisa

struts to the front of the class all perfect, and smug and cute . . . I mean, *I'm* not saying she's cute, but maybe there are a couple guys who think she's cute. Long, shiny, straight black hair, glasses . . . not cute in a popular girl kind of way, but cute in an *I can't get my head out of this novel long enough to notice you exist* kind of way.

I'm not religious, but I bow my head: Lord, with all your mercy, grace and perfect aim, please utilize your holy lightning to strike her down immediately.

There's no mercy. Julisa oozes on about the *me beneath this pale skin/The thousand vibrant colors of life under the blue-black ocean surface* . . .

Oh, Julisa, Julisa, Julisa. Must you?

She must.

Because she's Julisa Mendez. And she's the go-to girl.

Before the Seattle Supersonics got their asses stolen away, whenever they had trouble scoring, or the team was out of sync, they'd make sure and get the ball to their go-to guy, Ray Allen. Why? Because over time, Ray proved that he could put the rock in the hole.

Well, when a teacher at Puget High School isn't getting her point across and feels like nobody gets it or cares, she calls on Miss Julisa Mendez. Why? Because Julisa *always* gets it. She's always ready. She always has the answer. And it makes teachers feel less like losers when one person knows what's going on.

Orange-red fire looms unseen behind gray-black storm clouds of mountain rock/These are the shades of me . . .

I look around the class. Nobody's buying it. Nobody's listening.

I'm about to get religious again when I notice that some-one *is* listening.

Luis is holding his blue pencil and this teeny tiny piece of paper, and he's got his body curled up on his desk so it looks like he's catching zzz's, but he's looking up every now and then, and he's listening to Go To and taking sneaky notes.

As far as I can tell, I'm the only one who notices.

I snap my head back into position, looking forward fast. I'm not gonna let Luis see that I caught him doing that.

No way.

If he threatened to kill me for feeding him answers, what would he do if he knew I saw him looking all gaga over Go To's poem?

I don't wanna know.

Out of the corner of my eye, I watch Julisa walk by Luis. He immediately crumples the tiny paper and squeezes it in his fist. He steals a peek in her direction and plunks his head in his hands, frustrated-looking.

What is going on with this kid?

Taking notes during Go To's poem. No way that's gonna make any sense to me.

Ever.

I think about it awhile and come to the conclusion that he probably wasn't taking notes on the stupid poem. It probably didn't have anything to do with Julisa Mendez. I'm sure he was just practicing his gang script or writing some gang note to some gang buddy about who he wants to cap. That theory makes a lot more sense.

Still, I wonder about it for the rest of the day.

And the day after that. . . .

LOSING MY MIND

When Julisa smiles...

    Time
      Stops.

When she talks intelligent talk...

     My
    Heart
      Hops.

When Julisa looks my way...

    Whether at me
                Or not,

There's no

    Thought in my brain...

         Except

    Damn

       She's

            Hot.

—Luis Cárdenas

Dark Spaces

Every day I wear
The same
Stone cold
Cholo face
Hoping they
Judge this book by its cover

It's safer
This way
Hiding my secrets
In the darkest spaces
The unseen vaults
Of unreachable places

Shhhhh...
This poem's the truth
But you can't tell a soul
It's just for you
'Cuz I need you to know:
I got my journal
For good
Concealed
In the lining
Of my jacket's hood

My thesaurus
Is protected
Right where I locked it
Zipped in my backpack's
Deepest pocket

Folded microscopic
My New Words List
Sits under my watch back
Against my wrist

My mini copy
Of _Howl_ stays
Between two layers
Of socks
And my leg

And somewhere deep
Down by my heart and spleen
In my darkest guts
So they can't see
I lock the worlds of ideas
That make me me.

—Luis Cárdenas

CONTEMPLATING THE VORTEX

I OPEN THE DOOR TO THE HOUSE AND . . .

Three,

Two,

One—

"GOOD-BYE, SAM!"

Just like that, Gilbert's got me watching my mom's ghost fly past me, into the street. She opens her car door, then turns and looks at me for a split second. But before I can tell her to come back, she hops in her Honda and speeds away. A black cloud of exhaust smoke hangs in the air.

I watch it slowly fade away.

"A fine and pleasant afternoon to you, Samuel."

I close the front door and toss Ginny a grunt as I march to my room.

"All right then, kiddo," she says. "Don't mind me."

The way she says it stops me in my tracks. I realize what I just did.

But I can't undo it.

So I head in, melt into my mattress and hit the box.

It's "Scoff."

The drums pound like gunfire. I focus my mind on the lyrics. On the beat. The bass. Kurt Cobain's voice slaying the crowd at the Pine Street Theatre. I listen, and Nirvana takes me away.

That's how this thing is supposed to work.

Not tonight, though.

Instead of the music, I'm thinking about Ginny. About how I just ignore her all the time.

And I'm thinking about Gilbert.

Thinking about my mom's Honda.

About Luis.

I watch him run out the class. Watch him listen to teachers. Watch him work the Rules. I see Cassidy looking our way. She thinks about calling on us, then gives up and turns to some other kid and asks that kid the question instead.

It's unbelievable. We're going on two whole weeks since Cassidy called on Luis. Since then, she's barely even looked at us. Luis and I have pushed the Rules—pushed each other—to the point where we've created a time and space vortex, like we're there . . .

But we're not there at all.

I catch myself smiling in the dark, because after all the suffering and stress over Luis, it's fine now. He's the best seat partner I could imagine.

He still scares the shit out of me. But I can live with that.

I turn up the volume on the box and I'm back at Pine Street. The crowd is loving Kurt. He's loving the crowd right back, even though he's the kind of guy who would never show it. He smashes his guitar into the drums and dives, arms wide, into the mosh pit. The place erupts.

Then the video is gone.

And all I see is Ginny's sad smile.

It's clear sleep isn't gonna happen anytime soon.

'Cuz this Ginny thing is bugging me.

I head out to the living room to see what's going on.

Bill's in his easy chair, snoring in front of a blaring TV, a Fudgsicle-stained stick in his hand.

Ginny's popping in a movie.

She turns and catches me standing there and pretends to have a fainting spell. "You're up! It's SIX THIRTY—*P.M.* It's waaaay past your bedtime, young man!"

I almost laugh. Ginny's acting is really bad.

"Dinner's put away in the fridge. It's my famous green chili chicken chow mein. Just this once, I'll nuke it for you." She points her wooden spoon threateningly in my direction. "But tomorrow, by this time, you'd better be fast asleep, Samuel Ryan Gregory!"

She winks, just in case I hadn't gotten the fact that she was playing with me.

Oh, Ginny . . .

"And it's okay if you eat out here because it's movie night. We're watching a classic."

"Okay." I'm gonna stick this out if it kills me.

Ginny turns to Bill and gets loud in his ear. "Look who's up late, Bill." And she heads into the kitchen to grab my food.

Bill cuts off a snort and shivers awake. "Sam, you're up."

"Yeah."

"Did I tell you? Anderson and I are going fishing for steelhead below Snoqualmie Falls. There's a spot for you in Anderson's camper van. Of course it'll be riding low with all the snacks and sodas he's got loaded in there." He chuckles at the thought. "I've still got that slick outfit set up for you. Fenwick rod, Shimano reel. The whole bit. I've told you that, right?"

He's told me a hundred times. And for the hundred and first time, I tell him I'll think about it.

The movie starts up. It's *The Sound of Music*.

Ginny's back out with some popcorn, grape soda, and a plate of food. "It's a Mexican-Chinese fusion," she tells me.

"Ah, you and your fusion," Bill says.

"You love my fusion."

Bill smirks. "That I do."

Ginny winks at him.

Soon Bill's back to snoring and Ginny's talking me through the movie. "Maria's going to sew the children play clothes out of those old curtains."

Bill shakes off a snore, snorts and urgently sucks in a deep breath. Goes back to snoring.

Ginny crunches on some popcorn. "That is one resourceful nun, huh, Sam?"

"Yup."

So this is what seven thirty looks like.

I wonder what Rupe and Dave are doing right now.

THE REVENGE OF CASSIDY

"How many of you have heard of Langston Hughes?" Cassidy asks.

Julisa's hand shoots up. Her pencil sharpener flies through the air.

"Okay, Julisa. For the rest of you, Langston Hughes is one of this country's most famous poets. He was raised by his grandmother, in Kansas ..."

I didn't get much sleep last night. Thinking about the movie ... that nun, Maria, the von Trapp children and the captain, risking it all for freedom, singing their way over the Alps with a bunch of Nazis hot on their heels.

Seriously, how can you sleep after that?

So out of all the possible wrong things to do, I do one of the worst: I yawn.

I look over at Luis.

He didn't see.

I focus back on Cassidy. "Hughes attended Columbia University and struggled with racial prejudice there. He eventually graduated from Lincoln College and went on to become a major voice in one of our greatest artistic and intellectual movements, the Harlem Renaissance."

I can't help it. I yawn again. I feel my eyelids slowly close. . . .

I see that nun, Maria. She's got her guitar slung over her shoulder, hiking the jagged rock.

And I'm there.

I'm one of the von Trapp children, trudging over the snowy Alps, bare knees knocking, frigid in my leather suspendered lederhosen shorts. I look down the trail below and see a nasty Nazi climbing our way. I must alert Maria. I turn to relay the information, but she's right at my side. She says "*psssst,*" and she slugs me in the arm and I—

Bolt upright, waking up in Cassidy's class. I look up. Luis's eyes are wild. He jerks his head forward, commanding me to pay attention.

Cassidy sees the whole thing. She's talking to the class, but she's looking directly at us, pissed. "We'll be reading two poems by Hughes, 'Harlem,' from *Montage of a Dream Deferred*, and 'The Negro Speaks of Rivers.'"

I blew it! *What the hell was I doing?*

This is definitely it.

Cassidy's glare is fixed on us. She asks, "Boys, what do you think that means: *a dream deferred*?"

It's all my fault.

She lurches toward us.

Luis is gonna kill me.

Cassidy's a shark, shooting forward to devour its prey.

This is it.

This is the moment.

She kneels down in front of our desks and looks each of us right in the eyes.

Holy crap!

What is she doing? I'm sweating like a pig. My throat squeezes shut. The stinging on my face and pounding in my chest are unbearable. I look down at the ground. In my head I'm screaming, *GET AWAY FROM ME!*

She whispers slowly and seriously, "I'm onto you two, *Luisandsam*. And this thing that you guys do? This disappearing act? It's over. Got it?"

She taps our table.

And winks at us.

Then she goes on about Langston Hughes without missing a beat.

In mere seconds, Cassidy has exploded the vortex, and with that one-word name—*Luisandsam*—she collapses the magnetic force that separates the two of us from each other . . . and from her.

Without thinking, I look over at Luis.

He's already looking at me. Right in the eyes.

Rule number 4?

Gone.

His face is as red as mine must be. And we're both like,

What the hell now? We shrug and look away, knowing everything has changed.

Crap.

Luis breaks his blue pencil in his hand. He slides the
shards onto my desk.

Crap, crap, crap!

LUIS AND SAM, MEET *LUISANDSAM*

IT'S THE DAY AFTER.

I can't believe I'm back here after Cassidy's threats.

After I blew this thing for Luis.

He's probably gonna kick my ass, for real this time.

I sit down at my desk. He sits down beside me. I start bracing myself for the worst, but something takes me over.

I turn to Luis.

I look him in the eye.

And I say, "*Hey.*"

And before I can regret it, he says, "*Hey.*"

It's all Cassidy's fault! She's made us into a duo. Like we're a package deal: *Luisandsam.* She can put our names together all she likes, but believe me, we're in no way friends. And we'll never be friends.

But once you know the guy is there, and he knows you

know, and everyone else knows you both know . . . you can't pretend he doesn't exist.

So, despite everything, I say *hey* to Luis. I start saying *wazzup,* or at least nodding in his direction. In the halls. In the lunchroom. We even shoot each other a look when I pass him and his homies at Cholo Corner.

I feel fake.

But once you start saying *hey* to a guy?

You can't stop saying *hey.*

I CAN TAKE
CARE OF MYSELF,
YOU CRAPPY TEACHER

It's not just Cassidy up in our business.

It seems like everyone is noticing this thing with Luis and me. Noticing the *hey*s and the *wazzup*s and that sometimes, if we leave at the same time, it looks like we're walking to the next class together.

We're not.

But the whole thing makes people feel like they can talk to me. I mean, I'm walking down the hall one day and one of Luis's friends—this kid Willie—asks, "You seen Luis?"

Do I look like his freakin' keeper?

I swear, I don't know anything about Luis besides the fact that we both go to the same school. And all of a sudden we're pals?

It gets worse.

A week after *Luisandsam*, Mr. McClean asks me to stay after class.

I haven't said one word to the guy the whole year, and he's never even seemed to notice me. Now he wants to chat?

I don't wanna ever talk to him and I wouldn't be now if it wasn't for Luis.

I look back at McClean. He's one of these guys who wears short-sleeved shirts with double-wide ties and sports a big bushy mustache, complete with powdered doughnut crumbs.

He sits behind his desk and motions for me to come to the back of the class.

All superior.

I wanna take off and leave him sitting there stewing, but that would mean a call down to Carter's office and a phone call home. I have enough crap in my life.

So I walk back there to face the music.

McClean smiles and gets all hush-hush, like he has something important to say. He stares down at the ground for a second, then dramatically looks up at me. What a fake. "Sam, I'm concerned about your progress in my class. I don't have any homework grades for you. Do you have a plan to catch up?"

I keep my eyes on my boots.

"Everyone wants a future full of possibilities. You don't want a failing grade your sophomore year to hold you back down the road. Right?"

I'm not gonna answer.

"So it's time to make some choices. Choices about focus in class. Choices about completing assignments. Choices about friends."

What?

"The people with whom we associate have a huge effect on our level of success, Sam. You're choosing to associate with a kid who has made some extremely unfortunate choices."

"I'm not—"

"Sam, I know all about Luis's brother, and I know all about him." He takes a second to scan his grade book. Points his finger on a page of phone numbers. "I should call your parents about your grade. But I'm willing to postpone that conversation. You start turning in your work; you start associating with folks who will increase your chances of success, and I won't have to make that call. Do we have a deal?"

I look right at him.

I wanna tell him he doesn't know shit about me.

I wanna tell him it's none of his business who my friends are—not that Luis is my friend.

I wanna tell him where he can stick it.

But I can't.

I don't know why I can't defend myself.

I just can't.

So I walk out without a word.

Poetry Unit: THE DIAMANTE

Name __Luis__

Date   / /

Cherished Poets of Room 108,
    I know I teach you to be a bunch of rule-breaking rebels who can't
be contained within society's neat little boxes. So trust me when I tell you that
a few restrictions can actually help the creative process. Here's a type of
poem with a fun and easy set of rules. The *diamante* is a cool way to flip the
script on your readers. In just a couple lines, you go from talking about one
subject to writing about something totally different. Maybe the totally
different part makes a statement about the subject with which you started.
Sound confusing? Listen up RIGHT NOW! We're going to try some examples on the board. When we're done, write your own diamante below!
    Sincerely,

    Ms. Cassidy

1st Line: ONE Noun (THEME A)   **Mr. McClean**

2nd Line: TWO Adjectives (Describing THEME A)   **Lame, cynical**

3rd Line: THREE -*ing* Words (About THEME A)   **Nagging, sweating,
                                                              provoking**

4th Line: TWO Nouns (Related to THEME A)   **Cop, imposter**
          TWO Nouns (Related to THEME B)   **Teacher, role-model**

5th Line: THREE -*ing* Words (About THEME B)   **Glowing, inspiring,
                                                              guiding**

6th Line: TWO Adjectives (Describing THEME B)   **Awesome, smart**

7th Line: ONE Noun (THEME B)   **Ms. Cassidy!**

DIAMANTE: TWO SIDES OF A BROTHER

Rubén
Thoughtful, warm
Providing, singing, protecting
Brother, friend, stranger, bully
Lying, stealing, intimidating
Violent, cold
Flaco

—Luis Cárdenas

THE NEW DEAL

Cassidy doesn't whisper anymore.

She doesn't tiptoe around the two quiet loser boys. Now she calls us out repeatedly in front of the class.

Over and over.

Never letting us off the hook.

Luisandsam, are you listening?

Pointing her chalk at us.

Luisandsam, I know you're thinking.

Tapping our table with her long, press-on fingernails.

Luisandsam, where is your homework?

Glaring at us over her plastic glasses.

Be ready, Luisandsam. I'm coming at you with questions on this.

She says it and she means it. She's on our case from the second we walk in the room until we walk out the door.

Cassidy's turned into a rabid pit bull, hell-bent on breaking us, turning us into *students*.

That's her new deal.

And she sticks to it.

Every minute.

Every day.

NOT FUNNY

A WEEK AND A HALF INTO CASSIDY'S NEW DEAL, she shows no sign of letting up.

She's got the energy.

But we've got the willpower. We've got the Rules.

No matter how much *Luisandsam* crap she throws our way, we hang in there.

It's clear she's frustrated, because she keeps us after class.

She smiles and says, "Have a seat, guys."

I'm not gonna sit.

But Luis sits.

So I sit.

Then Cassidy throws us a curveball: *She's nice.* She offers us a doughnut—*from Krispy Kreme.*

That particular brand of doughnut is my weakness. But

I'm not gonna let her know that. So I don't accept. In fact, I pretend like the doughnut is the most disgusting thing in the world and it makes me wanna puke.

Luis?

He takes the doughnut.

Cassidy smiles.

He's an idiot.

She stands up and leans over the desk, looking down at us. "*Luisandsam*," she says, "I want to explain why I'm on your case."

I don't even have to make my eyes roll. They see the bullshit coming and do it on their own.

"You two are riding the fast train to *Loserville*. And if you get there someday, I'll be sad for you. Extremely sad. But I will not feel guilty. I will have no problem looking at myself in the mirror and saying, *Cass, you fought for those boys. You fought as hard as you possibly could.* So, *Luisandsam*, as long as you're in my class, I will not stop fighting for you."

We don't say a word.

So she writes us a pass to our next class. But she doesn't give it to us. She holds it up, so one of us has to take it from her.

"There's only one thing I hate more than a student giving up on himself. You know what that is, *Luisandsam*?"

I snatch the note.

"It's losing. I hate losing."

I slam the door on the way out.

Luis says nothing as usual. He just leads the way toward geometry.

I'm seething. "My God, she's a bitch! Right?"

It's the most words I've ever spoken to him, but he doesn't respond.

I don't think he heard me, so I repeat it. "Isn't Cassidy a bitch?"

And I say it loud enough so I *know* he hears me.

No response.

He just pushes the door open and flashes a ridiculous smirk.

I'm seriously pissed and he's smirking?

What's he smirking at?

Me?

He's laughing at *me*?

Just like that, he wipes the grin off his face and walks into math, his stone-serious, scary self.

What a psycho.

I swear, that's the last time I ask him anything.

Say anything.

No more *hey*s or *wazzup*s from me. That's it.

I give up.

I'm never gonna talk to him again.

LOSING

I FIGURED CASSIDY'S *HATE TO LOSE* B.S. WAS JUST A BUNCH OF B.S.

It's not.

She keeps her word. Each day she comes at us harder than the day before.

Luis and I both stubbornly follow rule number 7. (*Listen. Answer when called upon. Blank clueless stare on the follow-up.*)

And it stops working.

Because she never stops coming back at us.

Questioning.

Confirming.

Lecturing.

Heckling.

Taunting.

It's like we're the only kids in the class. Every stinking

question. Every new idea. Every chance she gets, it's *Luisandsam, what do* you *think?* She's relentless. If either of us gives a half-thought-out answer, she badgers us until we make it whole.

Every day the same thing.

She has us figured out and she knows it.

I hate her.

And I'm not about to forget whose fault this is.

Esteemed Poets of Room 108,

    More rules-driven poetry. "Ah, man!" I hear ya! Quit yer whinin'! This is fun, people. Here's the deal: If you're feeling a little bored with your poetry, and you need a little creative pick-me-up, try out this nine-line poem called the *nonet*! The nonet has nine syllables in the first line. Each line that follows has one fewer syllable, until you get to the final line, which has only one. It may or may not rhyme. That's up to you. Go crazy, kids! Try one out right now!

    Sincerely,

    Ms. Cassidy

---

9   Cannot think straight right now, Cassidy

8   You got my head spinning crazy

7   This is new territory

6   Could you back off a bit?

5   I just need to breathe

4   Get used to this

3   Attention

2   On me,

1   Please?

Nonet: Worrying for Me

Abuela holds my face in her hands

"You look like your papi," she sighs

Worries I'm too much like him

Too hardheaded and proud

She looks in my eyes

Tears glazing hers

"God made YOU.

Live YOUR

Life!"

—Luis Cárdenas

UNAFFILIATED

I'M SITTING ON THE METRO BUS, TALKING TO CARLOS FUCKING DÍAZ.

No, Carlos is doing all the talking.

It's what I get for not walking home.

This bus goes way down to main street Des Moines, down by the water. It takes me home the long way. Takes forever. I just wanted to stay dry on a piss rainy day, that's all. Just wanted a change of scenery.

But what I got was Carlos planting his ass next to me. And as usual, he's got Luis on his mind.

And just like everyone else, he acts like Luis and I are buds.

I tell him we're not.

He doesn't listen. He just goes off, agitated, real concerned-sounding. Like he's searching for answers. He tells me all this shit about how Luis's dad got shot in a drive-by when Luis was little. He says Luis's brother, Rubén, got jumped in not long after that and he's been in and out of juvie and real jail ever since. And he's probably killed a few guys.

Carlos stops talking and looks at raindrops running down the window. "It's why I can't figure this shit out. Those old-school dudes and his brother and cousins got Luis surrounded three sixty. Nobody really wants in the life, but man, it's in the air you breathe. It's in the water you drink. If you try to escape it . . . it's like fighting gravity. You can't do it. The force is too strong."

He looks at me as if I might have something to say about all this.

I don't have a fucking clue.

"Nobody seen Luis runnin' with nobody. Everybody got their eye on him, but nobody even knows if he got jumped in yet. Nobody knows if he's affiliated. And he don't talk to nobody, so . . ."

"What does that mean?"

"It means if he ain't affiliated, dude has got to get it done. *Callado's* a player from player blood. Everybody wants a piece of him. So if Flaco ain't got him runnin' with Sixteenth Street by now, then Deacons, Mafia, MS13, whatever . . . they all gonna come after him. And when they claim him or jump him in, who knows what insane shit Flaco gonna pull?"

Carlos looks at me like a life depends on what he's about to say. "I ain't gonna be in school for a couple days. You tell Luis I got his back. Tell him if he knows what's good, he gonna get his shit rollin'."

I don't know what to say.

"You on that for me?" He reaches up and pulls the cord for the driver to stop.

Carlos mistakes my shaking for a yes. "You okay, you know that?" He holds his fist out for a pound.

The bus comes to a stop and the driver yells, "Hey kid, this your stop, right?"

I want this to be over, so I pound him.

He takes off and I just sit there with my head on the window. I'm shaking like a jackhammer, wondering what Carlos's deal is. Wondering about Luis. Wondering what the hell is going on.

JUMPED IN

They beat you with their fists
Kick you with their boots
There's no shame
You take the blows
You feel the pain
It's all part of the plan
The day you're jumped in
And you become a man

Proud
You took the beating
Like a macho today
And you're in
You're in the gang
And nobody
Nothing
Can take that away

Hugs all around and you're free
To do everything they tell you
To beat, to deal, to kill
You're part of a special family now
But you've given up your will

I imagined that moment
For years it seemed
But last night
There were no kicks or punches
No screams
When I got jumped in

By the ghosts of dead poets
In a long, crazy dream

Shakespeare, Neruda
Ferlinghetti and Hughes
They shoved a pen in my hand
And made me pay my dues
Writing my thoughts and feelings
For days
Rhyming in all kinds of crazy meters
Getting to the heart of the matter

The fewer words the better
Because each one is precious
Each little letter

I wrote and wrote till my fingers bled
I poured out my heart
Then called to the poets:
    Am I in yet?

And Shakespeare said,
    I don't know, kid,
    What do you think?
    Are you one of us?
    Now that you've paid your dues
    Have you been jumped in?
    The answer, my friend, is up to you.

I woke up
And my decision had been made

So, homies and vatos,
No matter your colors
As of this date

Hands off
You're too late.

—Luis Cárdenas

THREE WORDS

Back in Cassidy's class.

I glance over at Luis.

He's looking straight ahead. Ready to take on whatever Cassidy is about to dish out.

I don't say *hey* to him.

I think about his psychotic smirking the other day. I think about everything Carlos said about Luis. And what he told me to say to him.

This is Luis's life. These are *his* choices. This is his deal. If people start coming after him, like Carlos said they would? That's on him.

I have nothing to do with it.

So I'm sticking to my plan. I'm not gonna say a word.

I turn toward Cassidy and sit up to show her I'm paying attention.

She says, "Listen up, y'alls. This is big. Poetry is written to be performed, so on March 8—three Fridays from now—we'll be turning the classroom into a *bohemian* café, and everyone—*Do you hear this, Luisandsam?*—*everyone* will be performing their brilliant work in the class poetry slam."

Does she seriously think we'd write a stupid poem for her?

I feel a tap on my shoulder.

It's Luis.

He hands me a tiny scrap of paper with writing on it.

It says *We're doing this.*

I look at him.

He doesn't look back. He stays in position.

I look at the note again.

We're doing this?

We're, as in we're both doing this separately? Or *we're,* as in we're doing this together? I look at him again. He nods in a way that says he wants to do this project *with me.*

I'm getting sick. I'm boiling over.

We're doing this?

I'm not doing this.

If I could speak right now, I'd tell Luis, *You scare the shit out of me. There is no fucking way. Why aren't you a normal gangbanger—the kind that wouldn't be caught dead doing a fucking poetry slam? Why do you think I'd speak in front of this class? I hate these people. I can't stand Cassidy. And what about all that shit McClean and Carlos say about you? What would make you think I'd want anything to do with you?*

The bell rings. I fly out of there.

I puke in the nurse's office and she sends me home.

BIG FAT STUPID JOKE

IT'S MONDAY. I have a plan. I'm gonna go to school. I'm gonna hold my shit together and not show Luis my fear. I'll tell him thanks, but no thanks. I'll be firm, but polite. And that will be the end of that.

The second I see him in class, I get a new plan. *Ignore Luis and hope the whole thing goes away.*

When I sit, he says *hey.* But he doesn't say one word about the slam.

Tuesday, I come to class shaking. I know this is it. He's gonna say something.

Nothing.

Wednesday.

He says *hey* again, just like any other day. No mention of poetry.

Thursday.

Nothing.

I finally figure out what that note from Luis had been: a joke.

Luis's idea of a joke.

I'm a dumbass for ever thinking he'd want to do *anything* in school, let alone recite some fairy poetry.

I'm relieved as hell.

I quit worrying about getting shot in a drive-by . . . or worse, having McClean call my grandparents.

Thank God.

THE ONLY WAY

FRIDAY I HEAD TO CLASS knowing I can forget about Luis's *we're doing this* bullshit and focus on bracing myself against Cassidy and her *Luisandsam* crap.

I take my seat. He's already there, in statue mode.

He gives the classroom a quick scan.

Then he leans in to me—dead serious—and he whispers, "Meet me after school. We'll walk over to my place and write the poem there. We'll have the weekend to get it on paper and two weeks to rehearse. The only way I'm doing this is if we completely kick ass on the eighth. It's the only way."

"Okay."

Okay?

As soon as the word tumbles out, blood rushes to my head and I'm squeezing a dry heave.

"You all right?" he asks.

I hold my stomach and lean my head on my desk. I barely get out an "uh-huh."

"I'll see you after school then," he says.

SCARED

I DO IT.

I meet him after school.

I go because I'm too scared not to.

But being scared is only 99 percent of the reason why I join Luis after school.

The other 1 percent doesn't have much to do with fear at all.

The 1 percent is made up of the following:

a) I'm bored.
b) Too many old people.
c) Curiosity.

Let's take these in order:

For starters, I'm so bored I can't stand it. I gotta *do*

something! This is the first time I've felt like doing anything in forever. And that's huge, because my level of boredom has been unprecedented. I've been so bored I don't feel like anything can be *not* boring. Eating, watching TV, going fishing . . . even listening to Nirvana.

I know there's more to life than this pile of blah and sometimes I convince myself to get out there and look for it. But I just can't make the move. I can't start.

I can't begin to start trying.

Until now.

I don't know why. I don't know what it is, but there's this little piece of me that wants to do something about it.

To try and get my ass moving.

The next part of the 1 percent: I'm spending too much time with too many old people. No offense to Ginny and Bill, but I'd like to hang out with someone who doesn't have her hair dyed bluish, or someone who doesn't have more hair growing out of his ears and nose than the top of his head. And it'd be nice to have a conversation with someone who doesn't start sentences with "I remember when I was your age," followed by a firsthand account of plowing the fields behind a mule or joining Pa to take up arms against the British in the fucking Revolutionary War!

The third and final portion of the 1 percent is curiosity.

I'm curious about Luis.

I wanna know what Luis is like. I mean, I thought I knew what he was like. I thought he was someone who wouldn't write a poem for stupid Cassidy. I don't know why, but I wanna know. And I'm curious to see where a kid like him lives. *How* he lives.

The fear of what Luis would do to me if I don't meet him is so big that this 1 percent of stuff doesn't even matter. I'd be meeting Luis if the 1 percent didn't exist.

But it does.

NOT GETTING EXCITED ABOUT WRITING POETRY

I MEET HIM OUT IN FRONT OF SCHOOL AFTER THE BELL RINGS.

None of his cholo friends are there.

No Carlos.

We start walking without a word between us. I'm freaking out on the inside, and I try to convince myself that I can back out later.

Could I back out?

What would he do if I did?

Okay, maybe I can't back out, but frankly, after what I've seen from Luis in class, I figure he won't have the guts to go through with this either.

Luis's apartment is a hike from Puget High School.

We walk up the hill a few blocks through the quiet, woodsy neighborhood that abruptly erupts into sleazy Pac Highway. Past a casino, a junkyard, an adult video shop, a drugstore, a 7-Eleven, a Taco Bell, and some old motels. We turn up the hill, east to the Viking Glen.

The Viking Glen is a typical boxy, gloomy beige, run-down apartment complex. We make our way around a plastic kids' slide, a couple bikes with training wheels, a *Little Mermaid* wading pool full of dirty rainwater.

It gives me the creeps.

I can't believe I'm here.

Luis walks up to a first-floor apartment, pulls out a key, and opens the door. He motions for me to head in.

Is it a trap?

I prepare myself for the worst.

The outside of the Viking Glen is a dump. But Luis's mom—or whoever—has this little apartment looking pretty nice. There's a big, gray, comfy-looking couch and a landscape painting of Mount Rainier hanging on the cream-colored wall, a full dining room table, and some bar stools at the counter.

Luis walks into the kitchen and sticks his head inside the fridge.

"Want something to drink?"

"Sure," I say.

"Beer?" he says. "Split a forty?"

Look, I'm no square, all right? But I don't drink alcohol. I've heard too many stories about my dad back in the day. So that's the deal with that. But now I've got a gangster offering me a beer. How do you not accept beer from a gangster? I mean, *come on*. . . . So I say, "All right."

Luis looks back in the fridge. "Oops, no forties, man. Clean out. And as far as beers go, we only got *root*," he says pointing at a can.

Luis tosses it to me. I feel like a dumbass.

He grabs a couple mugs and says, "I'll work on those forties for next time." He's smirking at me just like that time I called Cassidy a bitch.

He must have caught me looking the place over, because he starts explaining things.

"I live here with my mom. She's at work at the airport till midnight. Sometimes she works graveyard and she's there all night. My brother stays here sometimes, but he lives over in Burien. What about you?"

"Oh, yeah. I, uh, live with my grandparents off 216th, toward the bottom of the hill."

"How's that?" He says it like he's actually interested.

"It's all right. They're okay. Old. Really, really old."

"They know you're here? You wanna call them or something?"

"I guess I'd better."

Luis hands me the phone and I make the call.

"Grandma?"

"Sam, thank the good Lord! I just got back from shopping. I checked your room. You weren't back home yet. You weren't in bed. I looked all over the house. Sam, where the devil are you?"

"I'm at a kid's house doing a project for school. I'll be home in a couple hours."

There's silence on the other end.

Then, "Sam, that's great! Schoolwork on a Friday night! What's the project? Who's your friend—"

"Bye!" I slam the phone down.

Are you kidding me with the questions?

Luis has our "beers" on the little kitchen table next to a yellow notepad and pen.

And he sits there like we're gonna use them.

He's already written a title on the page. *Sam and Luis: The Explosive Epic Bust-Out Spectacular!*

"Serious?" I ask, trying not to laugh.

"Yeah."

"Look, I have no idea—"

"I don't either," Luis says. "I just wanna do this."

I'm panicking. I don't wanna piss him off, but the word slips out: "Why?"

"Why what?"

"Nothing," I say.

"What?" he says.

"Why you wanna do this?"

Luis looks at me like he wants to say something, but the words are stuck in him.

He looks down at the floor.

Up at the ceiling.

Takes a gulp of root beer.

Then he goes off.

"What if I go through life and I never say what I gotta say? Sure, Cassidy's a pain in the ass, but she wants to know what we got to say, and she's giving us a chance to say it, so what the hell? You only live once. Right?"

"I guess so."

He just sits there totally serious. Thinking.

I'm wondering what in the hell is going on. I'm wondering if I got anything I wanna say. We slurp our root beers without saying anything for what seems like forever. Then,

out of nowhere, Luis starts tossing out lines, clearly expecting me to fire back.

"*We're Luis and Sam and we're giving a shout-out* . . .
Sam?"

"What?"

I crunch the empty root beer can in my hands. I hate this
whole thing. But I make the decision to think of something.
I figure I don't have a choice. And there's no way I can say
anything dumber than what Luis is coming up with.

"*We're Luis and Sam, laying low all the time* . . . Sam?"

"Um . . . uh . . . Gimme a sec here."

"*We're Luis and Sam, and you don't know us* . . . Sam?"

Ah, fuck . . . I'm thinking . . . I'm thinking. . . .

"*I'm Luis. He's Sam. Something about something. No
plans* . . ."

Jesus! This kid is a freaking robot of talking. I try to
block his words so I can think. I squeeze out "*And . . .
we . . . we're sick of listening to you all, so we're bustin' this
rhyme.*"

"What? That doesn't go with *no plans*."

"I'm still on *We're Luis and Sam, layin' low all the time.*
I'm sorry. I'm slow."

He immediately starts writing. "*We're Luis and Sam,
layin' low all the time/Now we're sick of listening, so we're
bustin' this rhyme!*"

"*With words sublime, just in time—*"

"*Sublime.* That's cool," Luis says. "Sublime."

I don't even know what *sublime* means.

He comes back with "*To wake you up and blow your mind.*
Yes!" He's scribbling and going, "Okay, okay," and I'm

thinking, *This guy is crazy,* but all of a sudden, I realize I'm laughing.

I'm laughing.

We write crap like that, bouncing back and forth for a while. It's mostly posing, stupid, silly stuff, but we end up with a poem. And together, we read it back:

We're comin' atcha with fast-flyin' words
No lyin' you can't catch 'em 'cuz they're all a blur
So sit back, relax and wait your turn
Listen to Luis and Sam for a chance to learn
Yeah, we got words stored up for all you fools
They're flying atcha, no holds barred, no rules
Now that we've started, we can't take 'em back
We're a full-on slam, massive blast attack!

We look at each other like that was ridiculous.

But cool.

There's a shout from the living room.

HOME EARLY

"LEW-EE-EES! I'm ho-ome!"

"It's my mom. She's home early. Please don't judge me based on anything she says."

She pokes her head into Luis's room. "Hey, guys. You look hungry." She looks at me and says, "I'm Leticia. You hungry, Sam?"

She knows my name.

I look to Luis, not knowing if I should tell the truth or politely say, *I'm fine, we just had a snack.*

He turns to me and says, "Well?"

And she says, "Burgers?"

"Okay."

We get back to work—behind a closed door now—until Luis's mom calls us to dinner.

We have a seat at the table. I wait to dig in, wondering if we have to say grace.

No grace.

There are three big burgers on plates and all the fixings and some salad and glasses of water. Leticia hands me the plate and says, "Go for it, Sam."

I go for it.

Then Leticia launches in with the questions. "So, how's the project?"

I say, "Fine."

Luis says, "Good."

"What's the topic?"

I say nothing.

Luis says, "We're still in the planning stages, Ma. We don't want to blow the whole thing by talking about it too much."

"*Ay, tú,*" she says, reaching over and messing with his hair. Then she turns on me. "So, Sam. Samuel? Or Sam?"

"Sam's fine."

"How are your parents doing?"

"I live with my grandparents, actually. They're fine."

"That's good."

"Are they working?"

"They retired from Boeing a couple years ago."

"Ah. What did they do there?"

"Put *737*s together."

"Uh-huh. What team were they on?"

I look at her blankly.

She comes back with "Welding, interiors, paint, wings, engine? There's a lot to putting a jet together."

"I'm not sure."

"You should ask them sometime."

"Yeah." I feel like a dumbass for never having asked them what they did at Boeing for forty years of their life.

Leticia finally turns to Luis, but all she does is ask him to pass the salad dressing. "What are your interests, Sam?"

"Huh?" I know what she means, but I have to buy some time.

"What do you like to do for fun? What are you into?"

There is silence while I wonder why I'm freaking out about answering questions from a woman I don't even know.

They're waiting for an answer, so I say, "Music."

"Playing music? Writing? What kind of music?"

I decide I'm gonna say it. If she makes fun of me, I'll tell her it was a joke and say I really wanna be a software developer. "I'm into rock music. Bands from the late eighties and early nineties. Nirvana. The Melvins. Mudhoney, Soundgarden. I wanna play bass and write songs. I used to write lyrics, but not so much anymore. And I don't know how to play bass yet . . . but I'm thinking about starting that stuff up sometime."

Dead silence.

No response.

I'm an idiot.

Because grunge is dead.

And, come on! Who would ever honestly give a rat's ass about a random teenager spouting off about his stupid dreams? As I think it, I mentally air-quote the word *dreams*. Because *not* air-quoting means you're the kind of loser who goes around saying the word *dreams* seriously—like you believe in unicorns and fairies and rainbows.

Leticia slaps the table and says, "Go for it. It's never too late to get started on a song. And I'm sure there's a decent bass on Craigslist." She looks up and waves her arm. "I can just see you up on that stage, Sam." She turns to Luis. "Wouldn't that be great?" She looks right at me and says, "Do it, Sam. Do it."

I nod at her, like *I'm totally going to get started on that.* But inside, my guts are turning over because I can't believe this conversation is happening.

"You've got a passion," she says. "You should go for it. That's what I tell Luis."

"Ah, Ma, don't—"

"I tell him to figure out what he wants to do. As long as it's constructive, I'll back him one hundred percent. Isn't that right, Luis?"

I realize this discussion is partly about me and a lot about Luis.

"Sam, maybe some of your initiative will rub off on my *flojo* son."

"*Flojo*?" I ask.

"Lazy," she says making a face and poking him in the gut.

Somehow Leticia can get on Luis's case without seeming like a total *B*. I mean he doesn't seem thrilled with it, but he's not pissed off, either.

We finish up and take the dishes to the kitchen. Luis starts washing, so I dry. When we're done, I tell Luis I better head home.

He says, "Yeah, okay," and reaches in his pocket and whips out his phone. "You got a cell?"

"Yeah. No. Yeah, I mean." The truth is, Ginny and Bill gave me one for my birthday last year, but after a while of carrying it around and having it never ring and me never calling anyone, I started leaving it at home.

"If we're going to be meeting up and doing this thing, we need to be in touch, so . . ."

"I've got one. But I left it at home."

"You got to carry the thing around, otherwise why bother, right?"

I give him my number. He dials it and waits for the message to pick up. My message is embarrassing. I remember rerecording it a million times and never being satisfied. I can hear my muffled voice against Luis's ear. He doesn't react to how stupid it is, though. He snaps his phone shut and just like that, I've got a gangbanger's digits locked in.

"There it is. You've got my number, and I'll be calling yours, so don't forget to carry that celly, yo!"

We say good-bye, with plans to meet tomorrow morning.

I say good-bye to Leticia. She tells me I'm welcome anytime.

MUST BE NICE

ON THE WALK HOME, I think about what it'd be like to have a mom there for you. To razz you about your life. To give you a hard time. To cook you burgers. To be there. If not every night, then some nights. And on nights when she's not there, you still know she's thinking about your dreams.

HELLO, SAM

I GET HOME AND GO STRAIGHT TO BED.

But I can't sleep.

I don't know. . . . This stupid funk has been weighing me down for a while, so hanging out and writing some silly lines with Luis is the most fun I've had in a long time.

I'm awake in bed, staring into the shadows. Thinking about how I used to do this. I used to write stuff. I used to write lyrics in my notebook all the time.

Why did I stop?

I want the morning to come so we can get back at it.

I try to lock my eyelids and count some sheep.

I'm too amped up.

So I slip out of bed and walk into the living room and find myself standing outside Gilbert's cage. I watch him for a while. Watch him breathing, his black beak buried in his feathers as his little chest goes up and down with each breath.

Without thinking, I lean into the cage . . . and I start talking to Gilbert. I whisper, "Hello, Sam. Hello, Sam. Hello, Sam." In the friendliest voice I can manage.

Over and over.

Hello, Sam. Hello, Sam.

It's worth a shot.

Over and over, until I can't stay awake.

WAFFLES

IT'S SATURDAY. I got my phone in my pocket and I'm running for the door, trying to slip out like always.

But Ginny's standing at the stove.

In my way.

She's got one hand on a hip, a spatula waving in the other. Her bluish-white hair wrapped in pink curlers to match her pink sweatsuit.

She's damned perky at seven in the morning.

"Waffles?"

The knee-jerk *no* is about to hit my lips. Then I think about eating dinner with Luis and his mom. And I can't say no to Ginny.

So I sit.

In a second, she's got a hot waffle on my plate. The waffle is great but Ginny's smiling and bouncing around in her squeaky tennis shoes, asking all these questions about my new *friend*.

"It's just a project for school," I say. "No big deal."

That gets her even more excited.

"A project? Really? That's wonderful, Samuel! Tell me all about it!"

I can't stand all the *positivity*, so I bolt. I jump up and set my dish in the sink. "Thanks for the waffle."

I head out. But I don't get anywhere.

I gotta go back inside.

I gotta not be an ass.

I poke my head in. Ginny says, "You back for lunch?"

"Yeah," I say. "We put in a good five seconds of work and now I'm starving. You got a sandwich?"

"I got a knuckle sandwich, sonny."

"No thanks. How about another waffle?"

"There you're in luck."

I grab my dish out of the sink and by the time I'm sitting at the table, Ginny's got another waffle ready to go. She takes a seat and I ask her the question.

"What did you and Grandpa Bill do at Boeing?"

"Where did that come from?"

"Just curious, I guess."

"And did you want to know if I was single when I started out on the assembly line?"

"What?"

"Because I was. And I was a real looker back then."

"Okay, but what did you do?"

"I would let these couple of curls dangle down below the bill of my hardhat, and your grandfather, a strapping young buck working the crane, would see me walk in every day. He could view the whole factory from up on his perch. He kept an eye on me for months before he had the guts to ask me out for lunch. But he did it. He finally asked me out."

After a while, she explains that she used to check welds and rivets where the sections of the airplane's body—the *fuselage*—came together. It was her job to make sure that the welders didn't miss any spots and the riveters didn't screw up any rivets. Bill was the one moving those massive fuselage parts around the factory so folks could put them together. That was pretty much what they did for about forty years of their working lives. That and apparently flirt enough to make everyone in the Renton Boeing plant sick to their stomachs.

"I gotta get going now. Thanks."

"No problem. Thanks for the chat."

SUN BREAK

I START MY HIKE UP THE HILL TOWARD PAC HIGHWAY . . . in the sun.

Where the hell did that come from?

Halfway to the top, I stop and turn around. I look west, down into Puget Sound and over to Vashon Island. The view is an intense mix of colors. The dark blue water. Vashon Island's midnight green trees. And the whitest, puffy clouds. Winter in the Northwest. I don't know if it's worth all the days of depressing rain and gray for the few unbelievable hours a month that look like this.

But it might be.

I get greedy. I think about what I might see from the top of the hill. My heart starts pumping hard—in a good way. I rotate myself toward Pac Highway. I huff and I puff, sucking in chunks of air, hiking up as fast as I can, thinking this might be the most perfect morning ever.

It is. The mountain's out.

Mount Rainier.

Crystal clear.

The white snow popping the massive volcano's outline out of a bright blue sky.

This place is amazing.

MAKING SURE
IT DOESN'T SUCK

I GET TO LUIS'S. He says his mom's got to work all weekend, so she won't be interrupting.

I figure we're mostly done writing the poem. Luis looks tired, but he's way hyped, like he stayed up all night thinking about it. "We don't have much time, Sam. We have to make sure this doesn't suck. We don't wanna look like idiots."

"Okay."

"We can't just be rhyming to rhyme. We gotta be *saying something.*"

"Okay."

So we talk more about what we have to say, what we want our classmates and Cassidy to understand about us. And we end up laughing our way through the day. By the time it's over, we've thrown out what we had and we've got a whole new poem with a superhero theme.

I don't know if it's *great*. But I think it's pretty cool.

We huddle at the kitchen table and silently read what we have. Luis reads it out loud a couple more times. He seems happy with it.

"Are we done?" I ask.

Luis studies it. "Hard to say."

He gets up from the kitchen table and heads to his room with page in hand.

I follow.

He walks over to his closet door, opens it and disappears inside. Blankets and dirty clothes fly into the room. There's a clunk of stuff being shifted. In a second, he walks out holding a black-gray machine. It's a huge old-fashioned typewriter. It looks like something from a hundred years ago.

"Where'd you get that?"

"My grandpa died and left it to my mom. She never uses it, so she gave it to me."

"Do you use it?"

"Not much."

Luis grabs a piece of paper from the closet and puts it in the typewriter. He cranks the knob and the paper scoots into place.

"You got a laptop?" I ask.

"Yeah," Luis says. "In my mom's room. She lets me use it whenever I want."

"Why don't we use that?"

"I can't explain it." He points at the typewriter. "You just gotta hit a key."

He waits for me, so I do it. *Thwack*. An *i* snaps onto the paper.

"Feel that *pop*?" Luis asks.

"Yeah."

"Pretty cool, huh?"

"Yeah."

"You ever feel a computer do that?"

"No."

"That's why we're using the typewriter."

He pokes the machine one finger at a time, searches for the next letter, then pokes again. He squints, concentrating on the searching and poking.

The only sound is the metal arms of the typewriter smacking the letters of our poem onto the paper.

I go use the bathroom.

Come back and watch Luis type for a while.

Get another root beer.

Return to more typing.

Finish the root beer.

Go to the living room and watch Pat and Vanna. Then Alex Trebek all the way to Final Jeopardy.

I head back to Luis's room and wait until finally—*finally*—he whips the paper out of the machine. And studies it.

"Check this out," he says handing me a page. "Does it look done?"

I don't know what the hell *done* would look like. But I check it out and tell him it looks pretty cool.

"Really? You think it's done?"

"Yeah. I think so."

"I think so too. I think it's done . . . for now."

BOUNCE

We're finished for the day. I put my jacket on to go.

"What are you doing?" he asks.

"I thought we were done."

"Done *writing*. Now we got to be able to speak the thing backwards and forwards. If we aren't one hundred percent confident, it's gonna blow. No matter how good the poem is."

I take my jacket off.

We start reading the poem out loud together. It's hard.

But I try my best. I stumble along.

Suddenly Luis waves his hands in the air and shouts, "Stop. Hold the phone! This is *slam* poetry, Sam. This ain't old folks' theater." He smiles and says, "You're gonna put a guy to sleep with that kind of slop. Those words gotta *BOUNCE*, man! We gotta mean what we say and say it like we mean it. We gotta be rock stars! MCs, busting a funky flow with these lines. You dig?"

I do not dig. And I don't know whether to laugh or to run.

I look at Luis, and it's clear he wants me to do this.

So I decide to laugh.

And to try.

"I dig," I say. "I'll bounce."

We practice reading the poem until it's time for me to go home for real.

Luis makes me promise I'll work on the bouncing.

I promise.

He says, "Good." Then he grabs a pen and napkin off the kitchen table and starts making a little calendar.

"What's that for?"

"When slackers are feeling fine, that's when they sit on their useless asses and stop working. And, yes, I'm talking about you."

The calendar is thirteen boxes, one for each day until the March 8 slam. In each box, he writes the hours I'll be coming over to his place to work and the hours I need to practice alone at home.

"Who's the real Luis?" I ask him. "The tough guy I see at school? Or the royal dork scheduling my poetry practice on a dirty napkin?"

He's immediately serious. "Whattaya mean?"

"I mean, uh, you just seem really different than at school."

"How do I seem at school?" he says, sounding pissed.

"Nothing. Forget what I said."

"How do I seem, Sam? At school?"

"You seem . . . kinda tough—"

"Tough *and* . . ."

"And, uh—you know—not like . . . like a guy who would work on a project like this."

"Okay. Let me get this straight." He grips his hand tight on my shoulder and glares like he did when I stared at his scar. "What I'm hearing from you, Sam, is you don't think Mexicans can write poems or do schoolwork. Do I have that right?"

"No, Luis! That's not what I meant! What I meant was—"

I stop myself before I tell him, *You seem like a cold-blooded gangster at school.*

Then he points at me and shouts, "Ha!"

What the hell?

He holds his fist to his mouth, laughing. "Got you, Sam. I got you."

I force myself to smile with him.

"You shoulda seen your eyes," he says. "You were like—" He does a crazy imitation of me looking scared as hell.

"You got me, Luis. You totally got me."

He gives me the napkin and a pat on the back. "You're cool, Sam. See you tomorrow."

"See you tomorrow."

I take off, wondering what just happened.

Soap and Tears

I wanted to be you, Rubén

So I'd dress like you
    Walk like you
Get mad
    Tremble
Spit words like you
    Strike back like you

Accuse

    Accuse

        Accuse the way you do.

You knew I looked up to you
    I know you knew

You wanted it that way
    And I did, too.

Until the day I beat Mario
    After all those punches I threw

I looked in the mirror, brother
    And all I saw was you.

You, Rubén
Cold

  Hard

      Angry

        Bruised

And I heard the words:
    "Be careful what you wish for,
        It may come true."

I washed my face with the strongest soap
    And the hottest tears

Scrubbed off layers of you
    I'd put on for years and years.

Scrubbed off layers of guys
    You were tryin' to be

Scrubbed off primos and tíos
    And even Papi.

Then I saw myself in that mirror
    And introduced myself to me

It's been a while now, Rubén; I'm doin' fine
    And I think I'm ready to see you again

So when you've washed your face
    And only then

It'll be a pleasure to meet you
    And make my brother my friend

—Luis Cárdenas

YELLING AT AN OLD MAN

Sunday, February 24th.

I head over to Luis's for another day of work.

As I walk through the gate, I see him leaving an upstairs apartment. There's a super-old African-American man leaning out the door on his walker, pointing his finger at Luis and hollering in the rain. Luis hollers something back that I can't hear. The old man waggles his finger and slams the door shut. Luis hops down the stairs.

I don't know what to make of it. It doesn't look good when teenagers yell at old men with walkers. Doesn't look good at all.

Luis sees me coming and waits for me to get to the apartment.

"Who's that?"

"Mr. Graves. Family friend."

Is he serious?

"He's cool. We get in some arguments sometimes, but it's all good."

I make the choice to believe him.

SOLOS

INSIDE LUIS'S APARTMENT, WE READ THE POEM TOGETHER. I'm trying to bounce but I know I'm doing a shitty job of it.

Luis doesn't seem too concerned about my lack of bounce, but something is bugging him. He keeps stopping and losing focus. His head swivels, like he's looking for something.

I ask, "What's up?"

He sits there with his hand on his chin. He rubs his shaved head, goes *hmm* . . . and says, "Too much rhyming."

"You don't like it?"

"I think the rhyming is good."

"So we keep the rhyming?"

"Oh yeah, we should keep it. We just need to break it up."

He grabs a red pen and starts marking up the pages as

he talks. "We wrote this whole thing for the two of us to say together. We need to break that up too."

"How we gonna do that?"

"I'm pretty sure we need our own sections. Short poems. They shouldn't rhyme. We'll each write one and just stick them in there to change things up."

"But when we read it for the deal at class, we'll read those parts together, right?"

"No, man, that's the point. It's like a rock song with guitar solos. We're each gonna take one. It's your moment to shine, Sam."

I don't want a moment.

Bouncing is one thing, but shining is something different altogether.

I didn't sign up for shining.

I don't know what to say.

I don't mean to offend Luis, but I leave the room because this is crazy.

I go grab a root beer.

After it's been too long, he comes to the kitchen and asks me if I'm okay.

"Fine. Just thirsty."

"You wanna grab one for me, Mr. Manners?"

Now the gangster is all concerned about manners.

I grab him a can. He takes an aspirin bottle out of his pocket and washes a few down with a swig of root beer.

I look at him like that was a lot of aspirin.

"Nasty headache. Don't tell my mom. Mexican moms are the worst worriers in the world. Especially Mexican-American ones. So keep it on the down-low."

"I won't say anything."

"Sam, our poem is gonna be great. It flows. And that flow is gonna be even more ass-kicking if we break out of it then come back to it. You'll see."

I take a long sip of root beer. He can tell I'm not convinced.

"So you go home and think of something—*real short, no big deal*—and I'll do the same. We'll come back tomorrow and check out what we got. If it works, cool. If it doesn't, we can trash that idea and come up with something better. All right?"

I wanna say *no*, but I can't.

He makes it sound like it's nothing. Like it's the easiest thing.

So I don't say no.

I want to.

But I don't.

I say, "Okay."

THE BLUE NOTEBOOK

I GET TO MY GRANDPARENTS' AND OPEN THE DOOR.

"GOOD-BYE, SAM!"

Not now, Gilbert.

I head straight for my closet.

I dig all the way into the back and take out the backpack. Zip it open. Reach in. Root around, and pull out my old blue notebook.

I open it. The smells of Aberdeen and salt water and dirt smack me in the face. I think about writing back then. In the yard under the cedar tree, down at the pier, at the river . . .

I read some lyrics.

Some of my songs: "Fish Hook." "Jealous Teacher." "Bent Frame."

The lyrics are crap.

I was a punk writing stupid lines, trying to sound like a rock star and failing miserably.

But I wrote 'em.

I tried.

And goddammit, I'm gonna do it again.

Right now.

I turn to a fresh page in the notebook. I set it on my desk and put my pencil on the paper. I tell myself I'm not gonna pick this fucking thing up until I've written something to take back to Luis. I'm gonna sit here and do this.

MORNING

I WAKE UP AT MY DESK. The sun's back. A ray cuts through a gap in my curtains, reflecting up off the white page of my notebook, stinging me in my face.

I look down at the page.

There's nothing there.

I stared at it for an hour last night and fell asleep with nothing.

I look back up at that beam of sunlight. I open the curtains and check out the morning. Something about it makes me start writing.

When I stop, I've got a poem.

This sliver of sun
Slicing through curtain cracks
Cuts a hot stripe on my skin
Dragging me up
When I don't want to be bothered
Don't want to see, hear, feel, think.
This sliver of sun
Spreads like wildfire
And I have to watch.
I throw my glowing curtains open,
Feel a warm hand touch my face
Through squints
I watch the sun rise higher
Birds singing the soundtrack
As light paints the day with color
Like for the first time
I think I'll give this day a chance.

DON'T LOOK BACK

I DIDN'T HAVE THE GUTS TO SHOW LUIS AT SCHOOL.

I'm showing him now.

My heart is blasting.

He's got one hand on top of his bald head, the other holding my poem. His eyebrows are scrunched until he looks up from the page.

"I know. It's shit," I say, reaching out to grab my notebook.

Luis pushes my hand away. "Don't, man. It's good."

I don't believe him and he can tell.

"It starts bleak. And sad. But it's hopeful. And it's gonna work. Here's mine," he says.

I read it. It's about him liking a girl. She has got to be great, because in the poem he seriously wants her.

"It's all right?" he asks.

"Yeah," I say.

"You sure?"

I hand it back. "Yeah." He knows it's good. I don't know why he's asking.

He thanks me and says we should practice the stuff we wrote together yesterday.

A couple times through and my shaking goes away. I get the words out all right. Us reading together sounds good.

We get to the part where my poem is supposed to go. Luis stops reading and I know what he wants.

In a split second, I feel my throat go dry. I feel it close up on me. I cough it back open enough to ask Luis for a drink of water.

"Sure, man. No prob."

I hear Luis open a cupboard and grab the glass. I hear him turn on the tap.

I try my poem out. I whisper it to myself. I say the whole thing from beginning to end.

No big deal.

It's gonna be okay.

I can do this.

I hear his footsteps walking my way and I start shaking again. I hear Gilbert in my head and those kids from Rainier Middle School. Luis is back. "All right, Sam, let's hear what you got."

"I should probably write something different."

He's got two glasses. Gives me one.

I chug.

"It's good," he says, popping some aspirin. "It fits. Read it."

I try to read but my throat shuts down on me harder than before.

I cannot speak.

I hear Luis tell me it's okay. "Don't worry about it, man. It's cool. Let's go back to the top and read it all together."

He counts us off, "One, two, three, *go*—"

And I do.

I grab my notebook and bolt.

Because this sucks.

This whole thing is a crock of shit.

"Sam, don't—"

I head straight for the door.

"Sam, it's all right! You don't have to—"

I slam it and haul outta there.

And I don't look back.

CAN'T ESCAPE

I LEFT LUIS'S SO EARLY I'M IN BED BEFORE DARK. Just like old times.

"Floyd the Barber" is blaring. I try to see Kurt singing that song. Try to visualize crazy Floyd coming after Kurt with his razor-sharp scissors.

But no matter how much I try, this brain movie is all me.

Gripping my notebook.

Red face.

Open mouth.

No words.

Running away.

I feel cold coming in through holes in the blankets. I see light knifing through the covers, and I don't want it to.

I get out of bed and tuck my sheet and blanket in as tight as I can.

But I still see light.

I throw off my covers and get up. Swing the closet door open and yank out an old comforter and a wool blanket. I tuck in all corners.

I'm on my back, the blankets weighing on my face, soaking up my wet, warm breath—and, goddammit, there is still light in here!

I bury my face in my pillow and scream the lines of my poem until I exhaust myself and fall asleep.

MUMMIFIED

MORNING COMES. I can't move from my bed.

Ginny knocks on my door.

I tell her I'm sick.

I skip school.

I don't take a call from Luis.

Don't get dressed.

Don't even get out of bed.

Ginny comes back again and again; I just grunt every time she asks me how I'm doing. And I turn down all offers of sweet potato stew, Thai potpie, fruit salad, fruit leather, hot tea, iced tea, orange juice, NyQuil, DayQuil, Pepto, Vick's VapoRub.

I feel like a jerk, because I know that more than anything, my grandma wants to help me.

Luis calls again.

I still don't talk to him.

I think about my life too much.

And I wonder if I'll ever do anything worth anything.

THE NEXT DAY

BILL TRIES.

He opens the door a crack.

I tell him I'm gonna get up in a little while. I tell him *no*, I don't need to go to the doctor.

He says he and Ginny love me.

Him saying that makes me feel so small.

I can't say anything back and that makes me feel even smaller.

"You rest, Sam. You do what you need to do. But let us know if there's any way we can help."

"Okay."

He closes the door.

I pull the covers up. Close my eyes. Try to think if there's any way they can help. I can't come up with anything because I don't even know why I'm lying here.

The door opens again.

"I'm coming in, Sam."

Bill walks into the dark. He sits on my bed and reaches around till he's holding my hand. He puts a metal ball in and closes my fingers around it.

"Sam," he says, "I had this friend Alvin Johnson. An old-time Boeing test pilot. Everyone called him Tex. Tex was one of the first to fly the 707 prototype. Summer of 1955, it's his job to pilot the flyover for industry hotshots and all the folks at the hydro races at Seafair. Thousands of people. So he's got the big new jet over Lake Washington and he thinks, *Let's barrel roll this baby*. A full three hundred and sixty degrees. It's an insane idea, Sam. The 707 is too big for tricks. It was built to carry passengers. To make sure they get places safe and keep 'em real comfortable while they eat a baked potato and steak and drink a glass of wine. It's the farthest thing from a stunt jet. The thing about Tex Johnson: he's crazy. He doesn't care what that jet was built for. He wants to have some fun. So he goes for it. He risks his life and his job. But, Sam, he nails that three sixty. He rolls that plane in the sky above Lake Washington like it was no big deal. Like that 707 was born to roll. Then, for good measure, you know what he does, Sam? That lunatic rolls it again."

Bill stands and walks to the door.

"Word gets out about Tex's roll and people are thinking two things. They're thinking Tex Johnson is the craziest sonofabitch that ever climbed into a cockpit. And they're thinking about that jet. They're thinking if that big old 707 can do a three-sixty barrel roll, it'll probably do just fine flying upright to San Francisco."

He waits for me to say something. I don't know what to say about his story.

I feel the metal ball in my hand. "What is this?"

"A control knob off that 707. Tex gave it to me when your great-grandpa Charlie passed. I was real upset about losing my dad, and Tex wasn't much for talking to people about that kind of thing. Never knew what to say to me. So he gave me that knob."

He opens the door.

"I'll get out of your hair, Sam. But please let us know if you need something."

"Okay."

He closes the door and immediately Ginny's talking. I get up and open the door a crack.

"What do we do?" Ginny asks.

"I don't know." Bill sounds different than he did telling me the story. "I don't have any idea what to do, Gin."

"He deserves better."

"That's for damned sure."

"Why did Anne do this to him?"

"I don't know, Gin."

"What kind of a person would—"

"The girl we raised," Bill says. He sounds like he's holding back a sob. "Our daughter."

"We didn't raise her to walk out on her boy."

"We got to make it right."

"How, Bill? What do we do?"

"I don't know, Gin. I don't know."

I hear footsteps walking away.

"Bill?" she says.

"I don't know, Gin."

"Bill, we've got to—"

The front door slams. He starts up the car and drives away.

I close the door.

Crawl back into bed.

I don't know what to do.

I don't know.

I don't know.

PHONE CALL

I WAKE UP TO PEE. Stumble out of my room. Look in the bath-room mirror.

There's a photo stuck to my face, glued there by my spit. I must have rolled onto it in bed. I peel it off my cheek. It's that photo of Rupe and Dave shoving cake in my face.

I think about all the stuff I had going for me back then.

And I think about the fact that right now, I got nothing.

I gotta do something. Talk to *someone*.

So I'm gonna call Dave and invite him to my sixteenth birthday party.

Ginny and Bill said I could do anything and invite any-one. I figure we could go out to Aberdeen and pick up Dave and go to the Lighthouse Drive-In for fish and chips. Then some bowling or something. That's what we used to do on Friday nights.

I go to my room and pick up my phone. I still got his number in my fingers.

"Hi. Does Dave still live here?"

"Hey," he says. Even though his voice is lower than last time I saw him in Aberdeen a couple years ago, I know it's Dave. I know how Dave says *hey*.

It's my turn to say something. But nothing comes out.

"Who is this?"

Nothing comes out *again*.

I'm really getting tired of nothing coming out.

"Hanging up in three, two, one—"

"Dave?"

"Yeah?"

"It's Sam."

"Sam? *The* Sam?"

"Uh-huh."

"*Sam-bam frying pam!* What the hell you up to?"

"Not much."

"I'm glad I picked up quick. I don't think my pop heard, 'cuz if he did he'd be kicking my ass for taking a call at one thirty in the morning."

Fuck, I had no idea what time it was.

"*M. Night Samalam*, you drunk dialing me?"

"Nah. Sorry about that."

"No sweat. It's great to hear from you! You call anytime. Hear me on that?"

"Yeah."

"How's life in the big city? How are the geezers? They treatin' you okay?"

"It's fine. They're fine."

"Good, man. That's good. You in school still?"

"Yeah."

"It's all good as can be expected out here in lovely *Aberspleen*. I wish I was out your way. A little closer to the city. Get out and hear some music. Find some trouble to get into. Figure some life shit out. It's boring as hell, man. . . . Sam, it's great to hear you! You still writing those songs? Remember our talks back then? About starting a band? About all that shit?"

"Yeah."

"You doing it?"

"Nah. You?"

"I'm starting to, so shit's not *totally* boring. I got a couple guys and we've learned some songs pretty good. We played at this one asshole football dude's party. We rocked it pretty good. Then the scene turned hostile and some stuff got broke. We've moved on. The cool thing now is we're head-lining the grand opening of my uncle Vic's new barbershop— guess what he's gonna call it?"

"Floyd's?"

"That's right! Hey, we're trying to learn 'Set Me Straight.' You remember that song?"

"From *Houdini*, right?"

"The Melvins! Yeah! That album still rocks. Man, thanks for calling."

This is the spot where I wanna ask him to hang out for my birthday.

But the words don't come.

"Sam?"

Nothing.

"You there?"

Nothing.

"Sam, you okay, buddy?"

"Yeah. It's all good." I know I sound like I don't give a rat's ass about this conversation. But that's the farthest thing from the truth.

"Well ... jeez, it's been a long time," he says. "Hey, I better hang up. The natives are getting restless in the next room. You know, you should call Rupe up. I hear he ain't doin' so hot. Yeah, give that dude's ass a call. He'd appreciate it, man. You know he lives up by you now? Up in Renton. That's not too far, right?"

"Not too far," I say.

He gives me the number. We say good-bye and I know I'm not gonna call Rupe.

I'll probably never talk to Dave again.

Because I got nothing to say.

I go back to bed.

With no plans to leave my room.

BOXED SET

N<small>EXT MORNING</small>.

Ginny's yelling. "All right, hobo!"

I roll over and wrap the pillow over my head.

So she ups the volume. It's not a pretty sound.

"For the love of God, it's past noon and this is past funny. I'm coming in there if I have to break this door down!"

We are both fully aware there's no lock on the door.

"Make this easy on an old lady. This shoulder is not the battering ram it used to be back in the days when I used to batter rams!"

What?

"So open up or I'm calling in the Coast Guard!"

I get up and open the door. A brown paper package slaps my belly. It's tied up with string.

"That's for you."

I look up at her, but no words come out.

"It *was* a birthday present. Now it's an *I don't know what else to do for my miserable grandbaby* present. Open it."

I tug the string off and pull back the paper. It's Nirvana's *With the Lights Out* boxed CD set.

I can't believe she just gave me this. How would she know?

I look up at her. "This is cool."

"That's what they tell me."

"Who?"

"My people. I got people who tell me things."

"Thanks, Grandma."

"You're not going to slip away without kissing my cheek, young man."

She presents one cheek.

I do my duty.

She offers the other cheek.

I repeat.

Ginny grabs both cheeks in her hands, pulls my head down toward hers and looks me straight in the eye. Then, because it's her second favorite movie, she whips out her horrible Godfather impression and says, "Be grateful, my son." She playfully slaps my cheek the way Don Corleone would. Then she playfully slaps it again. *Harder.* "Be grateful."

"I am grateful, Godfather."

She marches toward the kitchen, thrusting a finger high in the air. "Thai potpie!" she shouts with commanding authority. "The egg timer tells me you're joining me for lunch in seven minutes!"

I can't wait till after lunch. I rip the plastic off the box and check out the CDs. The truth is I have most of these songs. But this collection has crazy garage versions and tracks Kurt Cobain laid down all by himself on a crappy tape recorder. If you really wanna *get* Nirvana, you gotta know this stuff.

There's also a DVD I need to watch immediately.

I go to the living room and shove the disc in the player.

Somewhere in the first few images, I see the craziest thing. I can't believe my eyes, but it's right there on TV.

I don't think it'd be a big deal to anyone else.

But it's a huge deal to me.

It's Kurt Cobain, Krist Novoselic and one of Nirvana's first drummers, Aaron Burckhard, I think. They're rehearsing in that little old house in Aberdeen. Or maybe it's after Kurt moved to Olympia. It's hard to tell. But they're rocking away, cramped in the back of a tiny room. Kurt Cobain is out in front of them, up against the wall. He has his microphone set up inches from the fake wood paneling and he's singing nose to the wall. His eyes are looking right into it.

Kurt Cobain is singing to the wall.

Is it because the room is too small?

Maybe.

But my first thought is he's singing into that wall because he doesn't want to be distracted by anyone. Doesn't want anyone looking at him. He's doing it because he wants to focus on the words. He's doing it because he's trying to not think about what anyone else is thinking. *That's* why Kurt Cobain is singing into a wall.

I cram down my potpie. Without thinking about it, I give Ginny a hug and a quick kiss as I sprint back into my room.

"You make a lady feel like a million bucks, then you run away from her like a bat out of hell? Ain't that the story of my life!"

UP AGAINST IT

I WALK RIGHT UP TO MY BEDROOM WALL. I cup my hands around my face and shield out everything.

I feel potpie breath bouncing back at me.

I feel like an idiot. But it worked for Kurt Cobain, so . . .

I start saying the poem but can't go on because this is so stupid I can't stop laughing.

This is my life.

This is what it's about right now.

Trying to read a poem into a wall.

Eventually I stop laughing. I get up and say my poem to the wall. I do it again and again. If Luis wants me to do this so badly, he'll have to get used to the fact that I'm talking to the wall. That's just the way it is.

Period.

End of story.

MY WAY OR THE HIGHWAY

I WALK UP TO THE DOOR OF LUIS'S APARTMENT.

I think about turning back. But before I can run, he opens up.

"Listen, Luis. I'm gonna do this, but I'm doing it my way. Up against a wall. If you think it's funny, then it's over."

He doesn't say anything.

I step inside, slam the door, and march into Luis's room. I walk up to the wall and cup my hands around my forehead and eyes. I breathe a couple deep breaths.

I deliver my poem line by line. Just me, my words and the wall. I finish it off and turn to Luis. "There!"

"That worked. Where'd you get that idea?"

"Kurt Cobain," I say, still facing the wall.

"Cool. Stay right there and let's do the whole poem."

But instead of starting the poem, Luis walks smack up to the wall and stands by me.

He cups his hands around his face just like I've got mine.

And he starts singing way down low, going *dom, dom, dom,* right into the wall. I can't figure out what the hell he's doing. Then it becomes perfectly clear: He's singing a Krist Novoselic bass line.

I join in with the doms because, of course, I know the song.

Then without a word or nod between us, we bust out our best Kurt together.

Come as you are, as you were, as I want you to be.
As a friend, as a friend, as an old enemy.
Take your time, hurry up, choice is yours, don't be late.
Take a rest, as a friend, as an old memoria.

Luis has it memorized.
So we sing the whole damn thing.
We blast that song at the top of our lungs!
Then we say our poem.
Complete with solos.
Right into the wall.

STEP BACK

THE END OF FEBRUARY TURNS INTO THE BEGINNING OF MARCH. We're back to our schedule with a week to go till the slam. Luis acts like the whole running-off thing never happened. He's only thinking about the here and now.

"I got an idea," he says. "Don't take this the wrong way. I'm totally digging the wall strategy. But there's not gonna be a wall in front of your face in Cassidy's class."

"I know that."

"So maybe you could try stepping back a few inches each time we do the poem. Step back and pretend you're taking the wall with you."

We go through it a few times. Pretty soon I'm a couple feet away from the wall and I start to get nervous. I put my hand in my pocket. Tex Johnson's knob is in there. I put it in my fist and hold it while I'm saying the poem.

"What's in your hand?"

"A knob."

I tell him Bill's story.

"That's fucking cool."

"Yeah."

"You're holding a piece of history."

"Yeah."

As we practice the next few nights, I hold the knob tighter with each step I take from the wall.

When I head off for home after practices, Luis is like, "Read and reread that third stanza" or "Practice those lines so you can *say 'em like you mean 'em.*"

It seems so important to Luis. So when I get home, I charge through the front door, ignore Gilbert's "greeting," head into my room and work my butt off . . . farther and farther away from the wall.

When I need a break or I can't sleep, I go to work on Gilbert.

I put my face right up to his and try my hardest to sound pleasant. *Hello, Sam. Hello, Sam. Hello, Sam.*

Then I go back to my room and Gilbert screeches, "GOOD-BYE, SAM!"

I don't care.

It feels good to try.

ON A TEAM

It's Monday, March 4th. I open Puget's front door. I get nervous thinking that in a few days when I open this door, it'll mean I'm headed to Cassidy's to perform with Luis.

I start working my way through all those rich Briar Park kids and I see this popular kid—Derek Hendrickson—putting on a show, walking like he's got a stick up his ass. He grabs his friend's glasses and puts them on his face. He raises his hand in the air. Waves it like he's drowning. "Ooh-oo-oo!" he shouts. "I know the answer! I know the answer!" It's obvious who he's making fun of. The kids all crack up. Derek stops walking and takes a big bow. The whole group gives him a round of applause.

I catch a glimpse of someone running away from the crowd. It's Julisa Mendez. She looks back as she runs down the hall. Tears are rolling down her face.

I feel myself burning up. I got my fists in a ball. My head's on fire. I swear to God, I'm gonna take Derek apart. I wanna destroy him. I wanna put on a show for all his friends so they can see what a weak-ass prick their buddy is.

But before I can get to Derek, I hesitate. The bell rings and he's swallowed by the crowd.

The moment is gone.

I stand there in the empty hall, playing the scene over in my mind.

And I realize that Go To and I . . . we're on the same team.

REALITY SUCKS

LUIS AND I GET TO WORK AFTER SCHOOL. We improve stuff where we need to—usually just making it sound smoother or less wordy, more bouncy.

We start reading some changes and there's a knock at the door. Luis goes to answer it.

This big cholo dude blasts into the room, freakin' agitated. He's my grandpa's height, like six two, and buff with this gnarly, black gothic-lettered tattoo that creeps up his neck out from under his white T-shirt.

"Wussup, cuz?"

"Not much, Frankie." Luis is real serious with him.

The guy bounces around the apartment, bug-eyed, looking for something. He opens up cupboards and drawers and messes up the place.

"Flaco here?"

"No, I don't know where he is."

The dude is breathing hard. He's got this sick vein pulsing red just below his eye. "Where's he at? It's real important."

"I dunno. You want his number?"

"I GOT his number, dumbass!"

Spit sprays when he talks. His chest heaves up and down with each angry breath. He opens a drawer and slams it closed with a *BANG!*

"He don't answer his fucking phone and I need to talk to him yesterday!" Frankie throws a book across the room. It knocks a painting off the wall.

"All right. I'll tell him when I see him, but I don't see him much anymore, Frankie."

"That's right; you don't see *nobody* much anymore. What's up with that?"

Frankie doesn't wait for an answer. He spots me and points a fat, trembling finger my way. "This your new buddy? You guys playing with your Pokémon cards?" He spots the typed pages. "What the hell is *this*?" His face is a huge, crazy smile with popping wide eyes.

He jumps at me.

I know I'm gonna die.

But Frankie doesn't kill me. He just snatches the poem from my hands and starts reading it out loud—mocking it—bouncing around the apartment again, spewing lines and howling. He drops onto his belly and pounds the floor with his fists and feet, laughing so hard he's got tears in his eyes.

"That's great, fellas," he says in his corniest voice. "Thanks for the entertainment."

Then he cuts the laughter and springs to his feet.

He hikes right up to Luis, chest to chest. He stares Luis directly in the eye. Luis holds his ground and looks Frankie in the eye right back.

"We all been wondering where you been," Frankie says.

All I can think about is Carlos and how he said people were gonna be coming after Luis. He said I should warn him.

"Now I know where you been. You been here writing poetry with your girlfriend. You planting daisies, too? Learning to sew? You hemming this dude's skirts? What the hell, Luis?"

Frankie bumps Luis with his chest. Luis bumps right back. "We need to know if you're with us, *Callado*. 'Cuz if you ain't with us, you're against."

"That's enough, Frankie. I get it. I'll let my brother know you stopped by."

Frankie explodes. "I'm talkin' about YOU now, *pendejo*! I'm pissed off at your brother but at least I know he's a part of the family. Don't forget who took care of you back then, Luis, who looked after you. We don't forget shit! So I gotta know—you with us? Or you against?"

Luis doesn't back away. He stares laser beams of anger up at him, looking like he's ready to throw down. All I can hear is breathing, then Frankie slams Luis in the chest, "Let's go!" Luis falls back on his ass. "Get up, pussy!"

Luis bounces up and charges Frankie, shouting, "I'm with you!" as he rams Frankie in the chest, knocking him backward onto the floor. "I'M WITH YOU, *CABRÓN*!"

I've never heard Luis even *talk* loud. Now he's yelling, barking at Frankie at the top of his lungs.

Standing over him.

Looking down on him.

Face red. Neck veins pulsing, his scar on fire.

Fists balled. Looking like he's about to kill Frankie.

Shouting him down. Saying all kinds of stuff about how bad he is, how tough he is. How he could kill Frankie right now and how he should.

I'm frozen. I can't move an inch, but there's an earthquake going on inside my stomach. What the hell is Luis gonna do?

He finally stops shouting. Everything's quiet.

Everything but the sound of breathing.

Frankie forces out a chuckle. "That's better," he says from the ground. "I was thinking you went soft on us, *Callado*." He reaches out a hand. Luis grabs ahold and pulls Frankie onto his feet. "You're getting strong, *guëy*." Frankie says it like he's proud of him. He hands the poem back to Luis.

Luis starts folding it.

But Frankie says, "Nah, nah. No you don't."

"What?"

"You gotta rip that shit up."

Luis freezes. "Come on, man."

"You choose, *hermano*." Luis just stands there holding the poem, looking as scary as Frankie. "You choose," Frankie repeats.

Don't do it, Luis.

DO NOT DO IT!

Luis slowly rips the poem. Shreds of paper drift to the floor.

"That's right," Frankie says.

Luis looks him in the eye the whole time, showing Frankie that, yeah, he's *with him*. And he's *made his choice.*

"That's more like it, *hermano*. Tell your brother I stopped by. We'll see you at Cristián's place next week?"

"Uh-huh."

"All right then." Frankie flings the door open and struts into the darkness.

Luis doesn't move.

A wet wind blows into the apartment. He watches the tiny shreds of our poem fly all over the room. He closes the door. The wind stops. Luis watches the papers float back down to earth. He closes his eyes tight. Rubs his head, acting like it's aching again.

"I don't think I can do this anymore," he says.

"Okay," I say.

Okay?

Luis grabs a broom. I watch him slowly sweep the floor. He dumps our work in the trash and walks into his room.

I wait for him to come out.

He doesn't.

"Bye, Luis."

I wait for a response.

Something.

Anything.

Nothing.

He doesn't show his face. He doesn't say a word.

He's made his choice.

AWAY

I walked this neighborhood—from Luis's apartment all the way to my house—the last few nights, and all I thought about was how good this made me feel. How cool Luis was. How he was the opposite of what people at school thought. How Carlos clearly had no idea what he was talking about.

Well, tonight Luis proved Carlos right.

Tonight Luis is exactly the person everyone thinks he is.

And tonight this place is scary as hell. Headlights glaring in my face. The shriek of screeching tires. Voices in the dark. Each sound is a threat that Frankie or some crazy gangster is gonna jump out and kill me.

I walk faster for a few steps, then break into a full run. I do all I can to get farther from Luis, farther from the stupid fucking poem, farther from trying, farther from caring.

Because when you *try* and when you *care* . . . that's when you get your ass kicked.

I imagine a big scar on *my* neck getting bigger and bigger. I run faster, all the way across Pac Highway and down the hill to my world.

To safety.

I burst into the house breathing hard.

"Samuel?"

I ignore Ginny.

"GOOD-BYE, SAM!"

I try to ignore Gilbert.

I slam my bedroom door. Bury myself in the covers.

I don't even look at the boom box. There's no escaping the truth tonight. Of all the millions of people in the world who could possibly be my friend, that thug was the best I could do.

It was never gonna work.

I knew that.

I saw the bloody train wreck coming from a mile away.

And I hopped on for the ride.

Who does that?

Lonely fucking losers. That's who.

INSOMNIA

Eleven o'clock
Can't sleep

Backlit
By street lights
The wavy tan patterns
In my funky curtains
Become desert dunes
And sandy trails
Connecting villages

In front of my nose
My dark finger bobs up and down
A puppet of me
As a desert walking man

I dodge rattlers
Outrun red wolves
Spy on enemies
Collect orange and red desert flowers
Visit my beautiful
Black-haired girlfriend
Who lives in the village
Beyond the canyon where the cold water runs

I give her the flowers
Kiss her sweet lips hello
Kiss her more
Kiss her good night, mi amor, hasta mañana

Like an old dust-brown tortoise
I lumber home
A million zillion grains of sand
Beneath my feet
An endless sky overhead
Infinite stars, infinite universe

I wonder about the meaning
Of my tiny life

Then picture her warm eyes
Her smile
Her hands touching mine

And I know I'm worth something
I know I belong

—Luis Cárdenas

WHAT DO YOU SAY?

AFTER A SLEEPLESS NIGHT, I WALK INTO MR. OLSEN'S SCIENCE LAB.

Luis is nowhere.

It's a relief. I don't wanna see him again.

I put on my lab goggles and yawn a huge one. I figure it'll be okay to close my eyes for a second.

One thousand and one.

I open my eyes.

I can't fall asleep in class.

But one more long, slow blink won't hurt anybody.

One thousand and . . .

The bell rings. My eyelids spring open. My cheek rests in a puddle of spit on my desk. I wipe my face and look around. I can't see because everything is a greasy blur. A brown blob flies at my face. I realize it's a hand. But I'm still half asleep and don't know what's going on. So I slap the hand away.

"Your goggles, dude."

It's Luis. He takes my safety goggles off and the blur goes away.

"You sleep-slobber like a hound dog, Sam."

I wipe my mouth with my shirtsleeve as Luis helps me up and hands me a stack of papers. "Here."

What the hell?

No freakin' way.

He retyped the whole damn poem.

Twice this time.

One copy for him. One for me.

It must have taken him half the night to remember it all—to get it right—and poke every letter into that typewriter.

Last night it was gone . . . gone with the freakin' wind.

This whole thing was over.

And now Luis is here. And the poem is back from the dead.

I don't know what to do.

He looks at me, then looks down at the ground like he's waiting for me to respond.

Then he says, "Sorry about last night. It won't happen again."

Locomotive

I'm a slow train
As I leave the station
Blowing my whistle
Kicking out steam
Rumbling down the track
Picking up speed

Got to keep pushing
Can't look back
Can't retrace the past
Or rehash your lies
Can't stop for talkers
I ain't got the time

So step back, haters
Get out the way, fools
I don't care what you're selling
Ain't got time for cool
No time for your kid games
No space for your noise
You can't stop me
That's not your choice
Your foolishness and loserness
Can't drown out this mighty voice

I'm a raging bull
I'm a hurricane
I'm a locomotive
So you can board this train
Or watch me blow past

'Cuz I'm never
Slowin' down
For as long as I last

To keep reachin'
New destinations
Got to keep goin' fast

Got to keep goin' fast
For as long as I last
Got to keep goin' fast
For as long as I last
Got to keep goin' fast
Got to keep goin' fast
Got to keep goin' fast
For as long as I last

—Luis Cárdenas

BACK ON THE HORSE

IT'S TUESDAY. Only three days to go.

I'm shaking as we take off for Luis's apartment after school.

Who's to say something like last night won't happen again?

We're at the intersection at 220th and Pac Highway, waiting for the light to change. Luis has his hands in his pockets. He's staring at his shoes. "My brother talked to Frankie. He told him to never show his face at the apartment, or he'd . . ."

Or he'd what? Stab him? Shoot him? What the hell? It doesn't make me feel any safer. It just makes it clear how messed up in that world Luis is.

"Frankie promised he wouldn't come around anymore."

I shouldn't be doing this.

I shouldn't be going anywhere near Luis's place.

I know that.

But what I tell him is, "Sounds good."

ROLLIN'

WE CRACK OPEN A COUPLE ROOT BREWS AND GET DOWN TO BUSINESS.

I take my spot a few feet from the wall. Luis stands by me. But before he counts us off, he points a finger at me and makes circles.

"We're barrel rollin' this baby. Three hundred sixty degrees, Sam."

It's so stupid it's great.

"Do it with me," he says. "Let's Tex it up!"

I make the circle with him and from that point on, we look at each other and do the three-sixty sign before every run-through.

We practice hard. We nail the transitions, the tempo, the unison starts and stops until it feels like we're so good we can't get any better.

Until we know we're ready.

I get my stuff packed as Luis puts the pages of the poem in our folder.

"Hey, Sam," he says, without lifting his eyes from the pages.

"Yeah?"

"Next time someone busts into my house and comes after me, you wanna grab a frying pan or something? I mean, serious. . . . You gotta have a homie's back, homie."

He looks up and starts laughing.

I start laughing too. "All right, *homie.*"

Luis walks me to Pac Highway. We see Bob's 99 Cent Burgers down the road and make a pact to celebrate with an all-we-can-eat burgerfest after we kick butt at the slam. We shake on it and I make my way across Pac Highway's four lanes.

I get to the far side and something tells me to look back. I turn around.

Luis is still there.

He's jumping up and down making the circle with his arm extended. He's laughing and shouting like a nut case. I can't hear him over all the traffic, but I know what he's saying.

I make the circle and shout back at him.

"Three hundred and sixty degrees, baby! Three hundred and sixty degrees!"

ANOTHER SHOE DROPS

I'm in US history waiting for class to start. I'm smiling like an idiot, thinking about how great the slam's gonna be. How Luis and I are gonna blow everyone away. How all morning he's been making the circle in class every time I look at him. He's been pumping himself up. Pumping me up.

Ms. Nguyen walks to the front of class and Luis still isn't in his seat. The bell rings. She gives us our assignment, and kids get to work.

I hear a *pssst* behind me and this asshole, Cooper, whispers, "You hear what happened to your buddy?"

I shrug.

"He's with the rest of them cholos. Fight off campus at lunch. Across the street. Blacks versus Mexicans. Cops broke it up. They all got suspended for a week." Cooper laughs. Mrs. Nguyen shushes him.

I feel like I'm gonna throw up.

We have this simmering Black versus Latino thing at Puget. It's stupid to call it that. It's only a couple kids on each side. They fight over territory—the bathrooms. They fight over who disrespected whom, and *someone looked at my girlfriend,* and crap like that. It's stupid.

I guess the whole thing finally boiled over.

I don't *know* if Cooper is full of shit. I don't *know* if Luis is involved, and I don't *know* if he'll be suspended, but, *come on.* Gangster kids are always talking about "having each other's back."

He isn't in either of our afternoon classes.

It's pretty obvious Luis was at the fight . . . with his *real* homies.

He made his choice.

If he isn't there tomorrow for the slam, I don't know what I'm gonna do.

WANNA KNOW

WALKING DOWN THE HILL toward my grandparents' place. All I can think about is, I wanna know for sure. I wanna know if he was in the fight and if he's suspended.

I wanna know if this whole thing is over.

I press the menu button on my phone and go to my contacts list. There's only one: Luis Cárdenas.

I snap the phone shut and shove it back in my pocket.

If there's something up with Luis, he'll call me. This slam is too big of a deal to him. If there's something going on—if he can't make it—he'll call.

Fuck it.

I pull the phone back out.

Ring. Ring. Ring and ring.

Hey, Luis here. Can't pick up. Leave a message.

"It's Sam. Just wondering what's up. We're practicing tonight, right? We should hook up one last time just to make sure we got this thing. Call me."

I hang up and walk.

And wait.

THE PEN IS MIGHTIER

What I used to do is
     I used to fight,
Now I don't
     Now that I write

Not that I don't feel
     The anger I used to
I still get mad
     About crap
          I can't undo

Bein' poor
     Too much rain
No dad
     Makes me insane
Stupid wars
     People who hate
          I still complain!

But not how I used to

When my anger came
     From my brain to my fists
No time to stop
     No thought to quit
Until I'd beaten someone
     Or been beaten myself
Left in tears of pain
     Or crying in shame

I don't cry like that now
        Now that I write
I battle on paper
        That's where I fight

I squeeze this pen
        And smash out words
Ideas collide
        My anger transferred

I'm in control
        I can take my words back
I can say more or less
        Explore gray
Where I had thought black

My words are trials
        or plans

Beginnings
        not ends
Births
        not deaths
Illuminations
        not fires

Where I had tried
        to elicit fear

I now hope to inspire

Myself

To work this stuff out

     And

Think
    Laugh
        Grow up
            Live

In a way that makes me proud.

—Luis Cárdenas

THE MOMENT
OF TRUTH

FRIDAY MORNING.

Puget High School.

Five minutes before the bell.

No Luis.

He never called me back. I haven't seen him since Wednesday morning, before the fight. He's clearly suspended.

I had held out hope that somehow he'd show.

You'd think I would have learned by now.

I've got years of practice with this hoping thing.

What I've learned is people are either there for you or they're not there for you.

And no bunch of hoping is gonna change that.

So here I am.

Alone with a choice to make. Should I go to Cassidy's

and watch the other kids do their thing and sit there pissed off at myself—and at Luis?

Or should I get lost?

The bell rings.

I take off running.

I'm out the front door, and think I'm in the clear. Then Carter sticks his head out the office window.

"Hey, where are you going, Sam? There's a special delivery for you in the office. Come pick it up and head to class."

I trudge back inside the building and into the office. Carter hands me a CD and a note. The note reads

> Hey, Sam,
>
> Sorry I can't be there. I hope you can forgive me. I can't really explain what's going on, but I'll tell you all about it soon. I know you're not going to want to do this thing by yourself, but I think you should. Do it for me. Do it for yourself. We worked too hard on this. I recorded my part on CD, so I'll be there with you. Just press play and do your thing, man! You're going to be great!
>
> > Your brother in slam,
> > Luis

Why doesn't he come out and say he's suspended?

As mad as I am, there's something about the note that makes it okay.

So before I know it, I'm walking to Cassidy's, CD in hand, running the lines of the poem in my head.

I pull the door open. It's dark in there.

Cassidy has replaced the fluorescent lights with candles. There's a spotlight outlining a stage. A music stand is set up for people to put their poems on. There's cookies and juice. There's coffee! It doesn't look anything like our class.

Cassidy strides my way with a huge smile on her face. "Sam, my man. I'm looking forward to hearing what you got."

It's wishful thinking on her part. She has no idea about the poem.

But she says it like she knows.

"Grab a cup o' joe. Sit back and enjoy. Hey, where's your partner in crime?"

"I dunno."

Cassidy hollers, "All right, gang!" She lays out the ground rules. "Listen respectfully. Fill out a reflection for each poem—respectfully. Stand up tall and speak into the mic like you deserve your classmates' adoration. And you'll get it. I promise you."

This girl Sherice puts her hand in a bucket and pulls out a piece of paper. She's about to read the first name.

I try to calm myself.

Try to breathe away the pinpricks in my face and the pounding in my chest.

Try to confront my fear like a man.

I can do this. I can stay and make an ass out of myself in front of everyone and be proud that I tried.

Or—

I bolt out of the room.

I feel freedom.

I feel relief.

I feel like a pile of dog crap because I'm a worthless fucking failure.

I start running down B Hall and Carter is there.

Again.

"Hey, where ya goin', bud?"

He puts a hand on my shoulder.

I wanna slap it off and keep running.

He says, "I hear it's big poetry day in Ms. Cassidy's class."

"Uh-huh."

"You better get in there. You might miss something."

"I need a second. I need a drink of water."

Cassidy's head pops out the door. "*Sam I Am*, you're on, dude."

Shit.

My heart's in my throat now. I swear I'm about to puke it up.

She holds her hand out. There's a cup of coffee in it. "Slam this. It's black. . . . It'll put some hair on your chest."

I chug it.

Cassidy sees Mr. Carter and smiles. "Forgive me, Carter. I don't have the sugar soda and Kool-Aid I usually serve the kiddos . . . just coffee today."

He's cracking up at Cassidy. I'm shaking like a jackhammer as I hand her Luis's CD.

"DJ Cass is on it. Pull yourself together, bro; I'm announcing you in ten, nine, eight . . ."

Carter slaps me on the back. "Get in there and do your thing. You're going to be great."

"You don't know that, Mr. Carter. You have no idea."

His eyes get wide. He's as surprised as I am that I talked back. "You're right, Sam," he says. "What I do know is you have a shot to be great today. I think you should take it."

I follow Cassidy into the room. I hear the whispers and try to ignore them. I step on the stage and face my classmates for the very first time.

I pull the poem out of my pocket, unfold it and place it on the stand. I don't look at anyone. I look over them. All the way to the back wall. I zoom in on that wall as hard as I can. I tell myself that it's just me and the wall. There's nothing I can do about what's going on in my chest or the pain on my face. *So forget it, Sam. Focus on your lines and say 'em like you mean 'em.*

Next thing I know, Luis's voice explodes out of the boom box:

Ladies and gentlemen,

Buckle your belts!

Take a hold!

'Cuz this jumbo jet's

About to barrel roll!

Everyone starts clapping and whooping.

Like they mean it.

Now, Sam, kick back and blast it, exactly as we practiced it!

I open my mouth and hear myself say the first line along with Luis. . . .

Superhero Super Slam

Sam and Luis:

I'm so quiet you never even notice me
I like it that way to go to and fro as I see
Fit—
Like Bruce Wayne in his Bat Cave
Like Clark Kent in layin' low by day

I'm quiet but test me, cross me
Harm my town or my family

And I morph, grow, change
I come alive, I rearrange

I'm Superman, strong as steel
I'm Batman cape flowin' out my Batmobile

Don't underestimate the power of the quiet
    ones
We don't say much but when we're under the gun

Stand back 'cuz although we started at zero
We go like ninety in two seconds like a
    superhero

Sam:

I've never said much, but with a lot of
    practice
I'm spinning the language, coming atcha with

Words that can describe or reveal the truth
Now I'm Clark Kent flyin' out my poetry phone
   booth

To save the day as Super Slam Man
I'm a brand new Sam, and a poet I am:

   This sliver of sun
   Slicing through curtain cracks
   Cuts a hot stripe on my skin
   Dragging me up
   When I don't want to be bothered
   Don't want to see, hear, feel, think.
   This sliver of sun
   Spreads like wildfire
   And I have to watch.
   I throw my glowing curtains open
   Feel a warm hand touch my face
   Through squints
   Watch the sun rise higher
   Birds singing the soundtrack
   As light paints the day with color
   Like for the very first time.

   I think I'll give this day a chance.

Luis:

I've been misinterpreted, misunderstood
You think I'm a thug, you call me a hood

I'm here to set the record straight once and for
   good
I'm livin' my life like a human should

Now I'm sending out my Slam Signal to alert the
   city
This vato superhero of rhyme can verse real
   pretty:

   The sound of her voice
   It's a lake when I'm thirsty
   It's a nine-course meal at snack time
   It's summer vacation on a January weekend

   It's never big or loud
   But when it's spoken to me
   It's a million-voice chorus
   Singing the words I love you.

Sam and Luis:

Don't underestimate the power of the quiet ones
We don't say much but when we're under the gun

Stand back 'cuz though we started at zero
We go like ninety in two seconds like a
   superhero

Flyin' fast, flyin' high with our capes on
No masks, we got our serious faces on

A job for Luis and Sam so don't stand in our way
We're comin' at warp speed to save the day

To make you feel something, to wake you up from
    your sleep
To surprise and entertain you, to make you
    think!

—Luis Cárdenas and Samuel Gregory

WHEN IT COMES RIGHT DOWN TO IT, I'M A BIG FAT BABY

THE ROOM EXPLODES WITH SOUND.

I'm frozen in all the shouting and clapping. This kid, Rashad, slaps me on the back and shakes my hand.

It's over.

I did it.

We did it.

It's just a classroom full of kids, but it's like I scored the winning touchdown for the Seahawks. In the SUPER BOWL! You can't hear yourself think, it's so loud. I just take it in.

And I feel it.

I feel it for the first time since I used to rock out with Rupe and Dave behind the Aberdeen house. *That* feeling. The feeling Kurt and Krist were going for when they named their band.

It's amazing.

I can't handle it.

I bolt out of the room again.

I'm feeling too much. I've got too much to say. I wanna thank my grandparents. I want them to know what I just did. I wanna tell my mom I'm not a complete loser.

I wanna tell Luis it was great. But I'm panicking, pacing back and forth in the hall like a crazy man. I'm breathing so hard and fast the blood rushes to my head. I got to lean against the wall to keep from dropping.

Ms. Cassidy runs after me. She wipes her eyes with a huge wad of napkins. Smears her makeup. Gives me some of the napkins so I can wipe my eyes. She offers me more coffee and spills some on her shirt. She says, "I'm proud of you, Sam."

I don't hate her anymore. I hug her.

I wanna erase the last few years of my life and start over right now.

From this moment.

Carter hits me on the shoulder with a rolled-up paper. "You killed," he says as he walks past us.

"You were in there?" I call after him.

"I was a witness to greatness," he says, disappearing into B Hall.

Cassidy starts punching me in the arm. "*Luisandsam*, you guys did it! You did it, Sam. I knew you had it in you! I knew it!"

"Thanks, Ms. Cassidy."

"Now I've got some butt to kick! I mean, where's that Cárdenas?"

"I don't know, Ms. Cassidy. I wish he was here."

It's great to hear people clapping and to see Ms. Cassidy all proud of me. But I feel guilty because Luis made me do this. Luis wrote most of the poem. He made me practice and got me ready. Without him, I wouldn't be here feeling better than I've ever felt in my life.

Next thing I know, Go To—Julisa Mendez—is standing right in front of me.

"That was great, Sam. You and Luis did awesome."

"Thanks."

"Where is he?"

I shake my head.

She looks down at the ground for a second, seeming genuinely disappointed. Then she pops back up with a smile on her face. "Here's my reflection." She hands me the paper. "It's all positive. When you see Luis, can you tell him I really liked it?"

"Yeah."

"And can you tell him . . . well . . . tell him I say *hi*."

"Okay." For a second, I think it's weird that she's talking to me about the poem, and about Luis. Then I think maybe she likes him. Or maybe she just really likes the poem. Maybe this is how kids who do stuff talk to each other.

I carefully fold the reflection sheet, put it in my pocket, and head back to class, smiling from ear to ear. As each nervous kid goes up there and reads, I clap hard. And I feel for the kids who freak out, because they got up and they tried.

When it's over, Ms. Cassidy gives me a pass to leave the room and call Luis. There's no answer. I leave a message. I tell him we did awesome. I tell him I wish he'd been there. He shoulda been there.

I try him again sixth period. No answer.

On my walk home, this thought hits me: *What if Luis isn't suspended?*

I start worrying about the stuff Carlos had said.

And I wish Luis hadn't been born into all this gang shit.

I worry about Luis's brother. About Frankie. About any other guy who might be out there fucking up Luis's life.

I got to talk to him.

MIRACLE

STANDING AT THE FRONT DOOR. I'm not sure if I can tell Ginny and Bill what happened in Cassidy's class.

Not sure I know how.

I open up and walk in. I look over at the kitchen. There are balloons. Ginny and Bill have set out pizzas and sodas and ice cream. It's like a corny little-kid party. I guess they had an idea about what was going on at school and they wanted to celebrate or something.

Ginny and Bill walk in the room. They don't say anything to me. Ginny just looks over at Gilbert and says, "Hit it, Gil!"

The bird starts singing, *Happy birthday to you, happy birthday to you . . .*

It's my birthday.

Ginny and Bill join in with *Happy birthday, dear Sa-am, happy birthday to you.* Bill pats me on the back. Ginny makes me kiss her cheeks again.

"Thanks" is all I can say.

"Thank your cousin," my grandma says. "He worked hard on that."

I walk toward the cage but before I can thank Gilbert, he screeches, "HELLO, SAM!"

Hello, Sam?

I know I heard that wrong.

Then he says it again.

"HELLO, SAM."

I freeze in my tracks and drop to the floor laughing. I can't stop. For the first time since the day I moved in here, he doesn't say it.

He didn't say it!

"Hello, Gilbert! How the hell are you, you . . . you beautiful parrot-cousin? You don't know how happy I am to see you today! Have I told you lately that I love you, man?"

I catch a look at myself in the framed mirror my grandma has hanging in the living room.

I look happy.

We all gather around the table to have our little party. My grandma hands me a plate full of pizza and asks, "How was school today, Samuel?" She casually tosses the question out as she passes Bill the pepper.

"It was okay . . ."

"Really, Sam?"

"No."

"Oh," she sighs. "That's too bad."

I look down at my plate of pizza, then up at Ginny's sad eyes.

I gotta tell her.

"It was the best day I've had at school. I wish you guys could have been there."

"That is something, Sam." She closes her eyes, smiling. Reaches over and puts her hand on mine for a second. "That is really something."

Bill busts out, "Sam, have a slice of pizza! You're going to starve. Eat as much as you want. We got plenty! This slice is loaded with pepperoni. Here!"

"All right, all right, I'll eat." I'm laughing like a dumbass.

We all sit there eating, a bunch of grinning idiots.

It's really nice for a while.

Then I get this thing.

From down deep.

The twinge of wanting . . .

I try to shake it off because this little party is perfect just the way it is.

But it's hard to fight the twinge.

I concentrate on smiling and thanking my grandparents for nothing in particular.

Or for everything.

When the pizzas and ice cream are gone, I go to my room and do some math homework.

Figure I might just give McClean a heart attack.

THE TWINGE
OF WANTING

HERE'S THE PROBLEM WITH GOOD THINGS:

When they happen to me, I think about my mom.

I wonder where she is—okay, I know she's in godforsaken Phoenix, soaking up all the sun she ever needed.

But when a good thing happens, I wonder where she is *right now.*

This second.

I wonder what she's doing. I wonder what she's thinking.

Is she thinking about me?

It sounds stupid.

But it's true. I wonder if she'd even recognize me if she saw me. I wonder if she cares one way or the other. So when good things happen, without her, somehow I can't feel proud. I can't feel all the way happy.

And when I can't feel proud and I can't feel happy, I feel

guilty as hell. Because my being down in the dumps all the time—being depressed and dissatisfied with everything—it's like shoving it in Ginny's and Bill's faces. Like telling them, *You're not enough for me. You're not good enough. You're doing a crappy job. And no matter how much you do for me, I'll never be happy as long as you're all I've got.*

It makes me feel horrible.

Because those two geezers are here for me.

Every day.

Feeding me. Worrying about me. Trying. Ginny and Bill deserve to see the good stuff I can do. And to see that I can be happy. So they can know they're doing good.

They deserve all that.

Instead, when good things happen, it's just pain followed by guilt. Followed by more pain. Followed by more guilt. It's a downward-swirling cycle of shit.

I'm sick of it!

So I'm vowing to change this thing. I'm gonna break the shit cycle right here and now.

And I'm gonna start by writing my mom a letter. I'm gonna tell her what Luis and I did so I don't have to wonder what she's thinking or if she's caring. I'm gonna tell her exactly what's going on.

Dear Mom,
How's Phoenix? I hope it's treating you well and that you're enjoying the sun.
    I did something good at school today. I think you would have liked it. . . .

WHAT IS IT?

I CALL LUIS'S PLACE SATURDAY. Sunday morning. No answer. It's like he fell off the face of the earth. I think of the note he left me. It's on top of my dresser next to the CD from the slam. I unfold it and read it again.

> I hope you can forgive me. I can't really explain what's going on, but I'll tell you all about it soon.

What is there to tell me about? That he's gone off and joined his brother and Frankie and Carlos's uncle and got himself jumped in and he's a real licensed, card-carrying badass gangster now?

If that's the case, I don't wanna hear about it.

Maybe that's not it.

Maybe he's got the flu and their phone isn't working. Maybe the phone's been disconnected.

It could be anything.

I need to calm my nerves.

I need to get to the bottom of this.

I need to do something.

So I grab my jacket and head up the hill.

Down Pac Highway.

Through the gates of the Viking Glen.

The place looks deserted.

I head toward Luis's apartment. I turn back a second and see these rough-looking black guys hanging out by a side gate, smoking. The way they're checking me out, it's clear they know I'm not from here.

I bounce up to Luis's door and knock. No one answers . . . *Luis, where are you?* I sneak a peek in their direction. Those guys are still following my every move.

So I book it outta there fast.

As I scramble my ass back down the hill, I wonder if they have anything to do with this situation with Luis. I wonder if they're from a rival gang. I wonder if they wanted Luis to be in their gang, but then Frankie got to him first. I wonder who they think *I* am.

And I worry about Luis even more.

HOW LONG?

I DON'T SEE LUIS ANYWHERE MONDAY MORNING. So I go to Carter's office and ask him how long Luis is suspended for. He tells me Luis isn't suspended. He tells me, "Luis wasn't involved in the incident. As far as I know, he wasn't even there."

Are you kidding me?

Where the hell is he?

BITTERSWEET DOUGHNUT

IN CASSIDY'S CLASS I TURN IN A ROUGH DRAFT OF A PERSUASIVE essay on voting. I worked on it over the weekend. She says she's looking forward to reading it.

I know it's not as good as it could be. And I want to make it better. So, for the first time ever, I ask for help.

"You got plans after school?" Cassidy asks.

"I do now," I say.

"Three o'clock. Do not stand me up."

I don't.

Cassidy is all business. Right off the bat, she reads a section and asks, "What are you thinking here?" I tell her what I'm thinking and she says, "That's good. Cross out the mumbo-jumbo and write *that*. Exactly like you said it."

I try it. She's right. It's better.

We go on like that for a while and about the time I think

my hand is going to fall off my arm, she says, "It's getting much clearer. You have some solid ideas, Sam I Am. Now go ahead and recopy your fixes onto a clean paper so you can actually see what you've got."

Recopying is the last thing I wanna do, but I don't fight her on it. I shake my hand in the air like helicopter blades to get the blood rushing again.

I'm barely getting started when Cassidy digs into her bag. "Doughnut? It's part of my see-food diet." She pulls out a Krispy Kreme sack. She hands me a big old O. I chomp it down. My hand feels much better.

"Sam, have you heard anything from Luis?"

"No."

"I called after the slam. I called Saturday, Sunday," she says. "I told Carter. I told the counselors . . ."

"I've called every day, too. Ms. Cassidy?"

"Yeah?"

"I'm freaking out about it."

"Me too," she says.

That's about all we can say. She gets to work on her teacher stuff. I work on my essay. We both eat.

And we worry.

LEARNING WHAT IT TAKES TO MAKE ME GO BALLISTIC

IT'S WEDNESDAY. Five days since the slam.

I'm working in school.

I'm trying.

The last two days, I've turned in my math homework. I've taken notes in science, been a responsible lab partner.

But the worrying does not stop.

I think about what it would be like if Luis were here. Would we be talking to each other? Would we hang out?

In McClean's class, I stare at his seat and lose myself in a daydream. I imagine the two of us taking off after school, talking about stuff as we head over to Bob's 99 Cent Burgers on Pac Highway. We order about three Bobs each and go on and on about how unbelievable it is that you can get a burger this juicy and great for only ninety-nine little Lincolns, plus tax. I picture us sitting there, dipping our fries in tartar and shooting the shit for hours.

Mr. McClean interrupts the dream and hands me back some corrected papers. He's smiling and extends a hand for me to shake. It creeps me out, but I shake the hand. He slaps me on the back and says, "Congratulations!" and tells me how great it is that I'm doing my homework.

Which is nice.

I'm happy for about half a second. Then something tells me he's not done talking and I'm not gonna like what he's gonna say. *Please, McClean, please stop right there.*

He can't.

"Sam," he says, "I know you like Luis. I do too. But you have to admit you're doing a much better job since he's been gone—without his influence. I don't think there's any coincidence there."

I boil over and explode on him: "You don't know one thing about Luis!"

I pause for a second and tell myself to stop.

But I can't.

"You have no idea what kind of an influence he is on me! You don't know him enough to like him or dislike him! So the next time you wanna talk to me about Luis, save your breath and shove a couple jelly doughnuts in your piehole and think about who influenced YOU and made you—"

Don't say it, Sam!

"Such a shitty teacher!"

We stand in dead silence for a second.

"I think you need to go to the office," he says.

"Yes I do," I say.

JELLY DOUGHNUTS

CARTER YELLS AT ME. But it's like *nice* yelling. Like supportive, yet disappointed and extremely frustrated yelling. He makes me wish I hadn't done it. But he doesn't make me feel horrible.

He does have to suspend me. For the rest of the day. And two days after that.

I ask him if I can go back and get my new assignment—another essay from Cassidy—before I take off. He's fine with it. Says he likes my initiative. As I'm walking out of his office, I ask if he's heard anything about where Luis is. He's serious when he says, "Nothing yet, Sam."

It's lunch. Cassidy's in her room alone. Munching on a salad.

"Headed home?" she asks.

"Yeah. I'm—"

"Suspended. I heard. McClean."

"He was talking crap about–"

"Luis. I heard."

"Who told?"

"Everyone, Sam. It's all over school."

"I'm sorry, Ms. Cassidy."

"Don't apologize to *me*," she says.

I collapse into a seat, pissed off at myself for losing it. For wasting my energy on *him*.

Cassidy rolls my way in her chair and slugs me in the arm. "Buck up, cowboy! Something had to be done, so you did it. It's over. Now, go home, get some rest, work your tail off on this assignment"–she hands me a paper–"and don't make any plans to run for office until you clean up that gutter mouth of yours. Got it?"

"Got it."

I start walking out, but there's something I have to say.

"Ms. Cassidy?"

"Yes, Sam."

"I'm sorry."

"For what?"

"For calling you a *B*."

She snorts a laugh and says, "Well, then, Sam, I'm sorry too."

"For what?"

"For calling you and Luis a couple of *F*-in' little *S*-heads on several occasions. So we're even."

I'm laughing now too. I hold my hand out for her to shake. "Yeah, we're even, Ms. Cassidy. As long as you promise to clean up that mouth of yours."

We shake. She reaches for her bag. "Krispy Kreme? I happen to have a *jelly* doughnut. Perfect for today. You think McClean might want one? For his *piehole*?"

"Nah. I think he might pass." I bite into the doughnut.

"Sam?" Cassidy says, sounding serious now. "I'm sorry Mr. McClean said that about Luis."

"It's okay, Ms. Cassidy."

"No, Sam, it's not."

"I know."

AIMLESS

I spend the afternoon wandering up and down Pac Highway, looking for Luis.

A couple kids from school—part-timers—are hanging outside the 7-Eleven. I ask them if they've seen him.

Nope.

I walk all the way down to the airport and all the way back.

I check out Bob's 99 Cent Burgers and talk to the Korean lady who owns the place and works the counter. She asks me what Luis looks like. I try to describe him. She points to one of her two Mexican cooks and says, "That him?"

I get home feeling like the day was a big, fucking waste of time.

But I tell myself I'm not gonna give up.

Maybe Luis is off being a gangster. If he is, that's on him and I can't do crap about it.

But if there's some other reason he's gone—like he's hurt or in trouble—I'm gonna find out what it is. Tomorrow I'm going back at it, back to looking for Luis. I just need a plan. I need a strategy.

I need help.

SNEAKING INTO SCHOOL

CARTER HAD ONE RULE WHEN I GOT SUSPENDED: "Don't come back until your suspension is over." *What's up with that?* Like the kind of people who get suspended for fights and truancy and booze are clawing and scraping to get back into Puget High School?

I guess it's not as ridiculous as it seems. Because Puget High School is where I am this very second. It's before the first bell. I'm standing just outside the front gate.

Why am I here? When I don't have to be? When I shouldn't be?

Two reasons.

The first: I need a photo of Luis.

The second: I need an ally.

Yesterday, when he escorted me off campus, Mel the

security guard said, "Kid, I don't want to see you around here till your suspension is over."

I peek inside the front door. Of course Mel is right there monitoring the texting cheerleaders from hell. He's wearing his drop-dead serious, *Don't fuck with me or you're headed to Gitmo*—which is what he calls his office—face.

So I decide to wait him out. Just then, my first-choice ally walks by.

"Julisa?"

"Hey, Sam."

It's obvious she cares about Luis. And we talked that one time after the poem, so there's a connection. Plus she's the smartest person I know.

I tell her what's going on. I tell her I'm looking for Luis and I need a photo of him to copy and hang on some phone poles. I need some ideas for how to get the word out that Luis is missing. I need people to help look for him.

She doesn't hesitate. "Yeah, of course, Sam. I've been worried about him. Let's get to work."

I tell her I need to get past the security guard.

"Mel?"

"The dude is a beast."

"Are you kidding me? Mel's a teddy bear."

She grabs my arm and barges in the door. "Hey, Mel, look who I caught loitering outside the building!" They joke around a bit, and Julisa tells him she's supposed to take me to see Carter. He says, "Yeah, sure, Julisa. No prob. You take care, now."

"Give my regards to your mom, Mel. She's in our thoughts."

"That means a lot, kid."

Just like that, we're on our way to Carter's office.

We tell Carter what's going on. He says he's working to locate Luis's mom, but hasn't had any luck. "Let's get that photo."

Julisa thanks him and says, "Well, I'm headed back to class. I'll see you in a couple days, Sam."

What the hell?

"See you, Julisa," I say, feeling betrayed, wondering why she changed her mind.

Carter grabs Luis's photo out of the big picture binder he uses to nail kids when there's a crime against school human-ity and the witness isn't able to match a perp's name to his face. Everyone's picture is in there. Carter makes a photo-copy and calls Mel to escort me back out of the building.

I ask Mel about his mom. He tells me his mother is a beautiful and loving woman, and he and his family are just sick about her bursitis condition.

"But Mom?" he says. "She won't let us turn this thing into a pity party. She won't have none of that. She just takes it like a champ. Makes me love her even more, which is near impossible."

I get past the gates with the picture of Luis.

But no ally.

I head up the road toward Pac Highway.

GREGORY, MENDEZ, AND DÍAZ

"HEY, GREGORY, WAIT UP!" Julisa shouts, establishing ours as a last-name-basis partnership. She runs a block up the hill to join me.

"You *in*, Mendez?" I ask.

"Yeah, I'm in. I told you I was. I just didn't want to advertise my truancy to the vice principal."

This is nuts. Miss Perfect, Julisa Mendez, is skipping school.

And it's my fault.

"What do you know about Luis?" she asks.

"I know that Thursday morning—the day before the slam—was the last time I saw him. He wasn't in school after lunch. So it's been a week. I've made phone calls to his place. Cassidy has too. No one answers. I went over to his apartment. He wasn't home. There were a couple suspicious-looking guys hanging out there. That's about all I got. How about you?"

"I barely know him," she says. "We just met in class this quarter. A couple weeks ago, he started saying *hi* to me every day. We chatted a couple times. Small talk. He's a sweet guy."

Julisa and I are two kids who don't know each other, setting out to search for a kid we barely know.

"You sure you don't have anything else?"

I shake my head. "That's why I got the picture from Carter."

"It's a start."

"There is one thing, I guess. One time when I was over at Luis's place, this pissed-off cholo came by looking for Luis's brother. When he left, he mentioned this other guy, Cristián. He asked Luis if he was gonna go to Cristián's place."

"When would he have gone to Cristián's?"

"Sometime in the last week. Maybe this week?"

"Any way to find Cristián?"

"Nah."

"Think, Gregory."

I wanted to do this without him because he's a fucking loose cannon. But I know we need him: "Carlos Díaz."

"Who's that?"

"This sophomore thug who knows Luis. He might know what's going on but he was suspended after the big fight, and I never saw him back in school."

"He might be back by now. Wait here."

Julisa's not the goody-two-shoes I thought she was.

What she is is an ass-kicker, 'cuz in a minute she's found Carlos and snuck him out of school. And she's already talked him in to taking the bus to Burien to check in with his uncle. The guy is a member of Luis's brother's gang. Frankie's gang. So he's gonna see if he can track down either Cristián or the brother and find out what's going on.

So Díaz is off to Burien. Mendez says she's gonna go home to scan the photo into her computer and make some posters. I tell her I'll help her, but she says I should try Luis's apartment one last time to make sure we don't do a bunch of work for nothing.

We plan to meet at Bob's 99 Cent Burgers in a couple hours. Before we split up, I give them my cell number just in case. They give me theirs and now I've got three names in my contacts list.

SUSPICIOUS BEHAVIOR

I TURN MY BODY IN THE OPPOSITE DIRECTION and head up toward Pac Highway into the glare of the one wet ray of sun managing to force its way through the black clouds.

Back to the Glen.

South past the Taco Bell.

Past the 7-Eleven, up 220th.

Past the cheap motels, past the rusty bikes and the plastic slide and the *Little Mermaid*, and up to door number five.

I'm relieved as hell that the two scary guys from last time are nowhere to be seen.

I knock and knock and knock—*dammit!*—and knock until my knuckles are raw.

I turn to go.

I'm halfway to the front gate when I see them.

Where'd they come from?

They're staring at me again. But this time they look seriously pissed.

On the way over here, I had convinced myself these guys had nothing to do with Luis. That they weren't really looking at me the last time. That I was imagining things.

But now one of them points right at me. And the other one takes a step my way.

I take a step toward the gate.

They take a step toward the gate.

I walk slowly and fake-confidently toward the gate.

They walk faster toward me.

I'm not imagining. I walk faster.

They start jogging.

I run.

They run.

"Stop, kid!"

This is it.

I'm gonna die.

I book toward the gate but they're on me.

I feel the imprint of chain-link fence on the side of my face as one of them bounces me off it. I spring back, onto the ground.

They're on top of me. One of them is on my back. The other one is pushing my face into the mud. I'm wriggling for my life and they're yelling, "Hold up! Hold up! Who are you? What you doin' around here? Snoopin' around all the time! And what do you know about Luis?"

Holy crap! They're after him.

"I don't know," I try to say.

"What? Speak up!"

"I don't know anything about Luis!"

"What are you doing coming around here, then, knocking on his door? Do you know where he is? What's going on? And his mom? What do you know?"

"I don't know anything," I manage to say with my face still mostly in the ground. "We worked on this project for school. Then he quit showing up. That's all I know. I'm coming around here because I'm worried about him."

"Serious?"

"Yes!"

"Aw, dude . . . Tre, get off the man's back."

He starts helping me up and brushing the dirt off my coat.

Tre says, "We're sorry, man. You just scared us, is all. Luis and his mom aren't around. Nobody knows anything. We thought . . . See, we was trying to get your attention and you take off running like that."

The guy that's not Tre says, "Man, that's some suspicious behavior! You got to work on that. *Serious.* All we're thinking is you're messed up in something bad and you know something about Luis. You okay? We didn't hurt you, did we?"

"Naw. I'm fine."

"We got mud all up on your coat. I will wash that mess up for you right now. *Serious.*"

They introduce themselves. Tre and Quintel. They tell me how long they've known Luis and his mom and how, along with Leticia, they organize the Viking Glen trick-or-treating and the block watch and all that kind of crap.

"We look out for each other around here," Tre says. "So we been trying to figure out what's going on with Luis and his mom. And worryin'. That's why we overreacted on you. We straight?"

I feel like a complete racist dumbass for what I'd been thinking about them. For the reasons I ran. "Yeah, that's fine. I'm sorry I ran away from you."

"No problem. Come around here anytime, Sam. You should go meet old man Graves. Luis and his mom check in on him all the time, so he's pretty worried." Tre points up the stairs. "Apartment twenty-three."

BANANA BREAD

I KNOCK.

There's yelling.

"Hold on! Hold on! Don't go away! Graves is coming! Not in the *grave* yet—ha-ha!"

It's like the door is made of paper, I can hear him so well. The old man opens up. He's little. He must weigh a hundred and ten pounds or something. He might be a hundred and ten years old, too. He has a bald head and a huge toothy smile. The sweet smell of banana bread smacks me in the face.

"Hey, friend, state your name. Speak up, now."

"Sam Gregory. I'm a friend of Luis Cárdenas."

"In that case, come on in!"

We shake hands. I can feel every bone, he's so skinny.

I walk into the tiny cluttered apartment and see pictures of Jesus and Martin Luther King and all these leaders on the wall. The Kennedys, Rosa Parks, Cesar Chavez. There's a bunch of other important-looking people I can't name. And pictures of people who must be Graves's family. There are newspapers everywhere and clippings on the fridge and coffee table.

"Where's Luis?" Graves asks me.

"I was hoping you would know."

"My daughter came into town and took me to the ocean for a few days. I just got back this morning. They tell me Luis and Leticia have been gone for a week. Not sure what's going on there. I do know they'll check in when they get back. They never let too long go by without a visit."

A buzzer goes off.

"My bread! Can I interest you in some of my hot banana bread? It's award-winning bread, son."

"Sure." I haven't eaten all day. It takes him about a year to get into the kitchen and cut the bread.

He talks the whole time. Tells me about when he was in the hospital after breaking a hip. Leticia helped him use the facilities when he couldn't get a nurse to answer the call. "She was visiting the hospital. Just walking by. Didn't know me from Adam," he says. Leticia realized he didn't have any family around so she checked up on him every day while he was in there. "We been friends ever since," he says. "I even pulled strings with the manager to help her get the apartment. We're that way. Helping each other out."

Graves pulls the knife out of the bread and tears off a sheet of foil.

"So you're friends with Luis?" he asks.

"Yeah. We worked on this project together."

"Real smart boy. He drops in and we talk about the state of the world. Mostly I do the talking. Sometimes he disagrees with me and I give him a piece of my mind." Graves laughs. "We get into it but we fight fair. I give him some bread or my famous coconut cookies. He fetches my mail. Runs to the store for my eggs and coffee. Looks in on me every couple days."

"I haven't seen him for over a week. I'm looking for him, though. I think I better get going, Mr. Graves."

"Not without your bread." He carefully wraps the big hunk of bread, folding the foil into hospital corners. He hands me the piping-hot package and a smaller piece wrapped in a paper towel.

"There's one for the road."

"Thanks, Mr. Graves. You need anything?"

"No, son. I'm fine."

"All right."

I start to head out but he says, "Wait. I take that back. I'm not fine until I know what's going on with Luis and Leticia. So what I need is for you to keep on searching. And call me if you find out anything."

"Will do. What's your number?" Again with the cell phone. I type in *Graves* and add him to my contacts.

He pats my shoulder and says, "See you again, son." He says it like he really wants to.

"See you," I say back.

I head out and rip into the foil because Graves's bread is so good and I'm so hungry. The whole thing is gone before I'm two blocks away.

BOB'S

WHEN I GET THERE, Julisa's sitting at a table behind a big stack of bright orange flyers with a decent photocopy of Luis's mug on them. She's marking up a map. Chewing on some onion rings.

"Gregory, grab some sustenance."

I dip a ring into some tartar sauce and take a seat. I tell her about Graves and Quintel and Tre. I tell her we're not the only ones worried about Luis.

Carlos bursts through the door and sits beside us.

"You got anything, Díaz?" Julisa asks.

"My cousin said he was at Cristián's and Luis was a no-show. *Vatos* were real pissed. But it's nothing new 'cuz it's been a long time since Luis hung with anybody. The crazier thing is nobody's seen Flaco in a whole week. That crew is tight and nobody knows nothing."

I tell him to keep on asking around. He seems gung-ho to help out.

We both look to Julisa. "All right, guys. Let's get rolling on the posters." She grabs her big old pencil pouch and selects the proper highlighter, highlighting our individual territories on our maps. She gives us a stack of posters. She's got a staple gun and a couple hammers and nails, so we're covered there.

Before we split up, Julisa asks where we should meet in the morning.

"You're in for another day?" I ask.

"I don't see Luis anywhere," she says.

I like Julisa Mendez.

As we walk out, the Korean lady wishes us good luck.

Carlos stops just outside the door. "I never mentioned this 'cuz I just remembered it. This one time a few months ago, my little brother, Aldo, told me Luis was at his school, hangin' out in the next class or something. I don't know what he was doing over there, but I think it's strange. Gangster hangin' out at an elementary school."

"Did you ever ask him about it?" I say.

"Nah, man. We don't talk much."

"Do you guys talk ever?"

"He got his own thing."

"You talked like you knew him."

"We're not pals, awright? But everyone knows all kinds of shit about his brother. And about his pop. But Luis? He don't really talk to nobody. He's a mystery dude."

"Do you know how he got his scar?"

"Nah, but I can imagine. There are all kinds of stories

out there, but nobody knows for sure. What I do know is bad *vatos* get bad scars."

I finally get it. All that time when I thought Carlos knew him, when he was bugging me about him, he was just trying to get closer to Luis. He doesn't know him at all.

"So which elementary school did your brother see him at?"

"Denny, man."

I tell them I'm going over there after school tomorrow.

We head into the rain our separate ways and start getting acquainted with the phone poles of Des Moines, Washington.

STUFF A MOTHER SHOULD KNOW

I EAT DINNER WITH GINNY AND BILL.

I can't tell them I'm suspended and this whole thing with Luis is too intense to talk about.

They couldn't do anything about it anyway.

They could worry.

But I'm doing enough of that already.

Ginny asks me if I'm okay. I tell her I'm fine. That's about all that gets said. In all the quiet, I wonder if I'd be telling my mom everything if she were here.

I think about the letter I started the night of the slam. It's sitting there on my bed waiting for me. So I decide to finish it.

I tell my mom about Luis and the poetry slam and I can't stop writing. I feel this need to tell her every good thing I've ever done.

I write about doing my homework in Cassidy's class. In McClean's class. Nguyen's class. I write about mowing the lawn all last summer. Ours and the neighbor's. I write about the time I caught a sixteen-inch sea-run cutthroat trout fishing with Bill my first summer here. I tell her I had perfect attendance last year.

I know there's more.

I go to the closet and pull out the backpack. Besides old pictures, I stuffed every certificate or sticker or award I ever got in there. I've never taken any of them out.

Until now.

There's a "Citizen of the Week" award from June 2 to June 6 my fifth-grade year. There's one for a fourth-grade spelling bee. I pull out a note from my third-grade teacher thanking me for helping her put the chairs up after school. There's a Defensive Co-MVP medal from my U-10 soccer team and one for "Extraordinary Service" to the Audio-Visual Squad from sixth grade.

Most of this stuff happened before she left me here. I don't care. I put it all in the letter. I can't stop writing. I list everything in the pack. Everything in my memory. I fold the letter and stick it in an envelope. Address it. Stamp it. Shove it in my pocket.

I need my mom to know this stuff.

RUPE

Can't sleep.

I go to my dresser and pull out the scrap of paper. It's Rupe's number from when I talked to Dave. I try it. There's an answer on the other end. "Rupert?"

It's not Rupe but the voice on the other end says he'll get him.

"Yeah?"

"It's Sam, Rupe. Dave gave me your number."

"Are you serious? Sam? God, it's good to hear from you."

"You okay, Rupe?"

"I'm gettin' there."

I listen to his crazy stuff. Dave was right. Rupe isn't doing so hot. He's out of school and living with a friend. Rupe's mom died when we were little. Now his dad is sick. Apparently, Rupe fucked up enough that his dad kicked him out. He tells me he's in teen Alcoholics Anonymous trying to get his shit together.

He says sorry for some dumb stuff I don't even remember from when we were kids and for not calling me back when I tried to get ahold of him a long time ago.

I tell him he doesn't have to say sorry. I tell him it's no big deal.

He tells me it's a big deal to him.

I ask Rupe for help.

He checks the bus schedule and says he'll see me in the morning.

We hang up and I punch Rupe's name into my contacts list.

LOOKING FOR LUIS
IN SECOND GRADE

THERE'S NO WAY I'D BE THIS FAR WITHOUT JULISA. If I ever feel like changing the world for the better, there is no doubt about it, Julisa Mendez will be my *go-to girl*.

By two o'clock Friday, she's made sure that Carlos, Rupe, and I have every telephone pole on every major street in Des Moines covered. She's called four news stations and the *Seattle Times*. And the cops. They tell her the assistant principal from Puget High already filed the report. That's Carter. It's good to know we're not alone on this.

Now she and the guys are off knocking on doors in the neighborhoods surrounding Viking Glen and I'm at Denny Elementary.

School's just ended. I tell some little kids I'm looking for Aldo Díaz. They point out this cute owl-eyed little guy who in no way looks like a gangster's brother. I tell him I know Carlos and he tells me his teacher is Ms. Gilmore.

Ms. Gilmore's class is at the very end of the hall. The sign on the door next to hers reads *Mrs. Peña, 2nd Grade*. I peek inside. It doesn't look like anyone is in there.

I knock.

Nothing.

There's a bench across from her door so I take a seat and start thinking.

What the hell am I doing here?

I get up and peek in at the classroom walls, trying to remember what it was like to be a second grader. I can't remember much. I know I did well in school then. I guess I was a typical kid. I lived for recess. I was always building stuff and loved listening to my second-grade teacher, Mrs. Towner, reading Dr. Seuss books in her funny voices. She was awesome. I remember we raised baby Coho in tanks and when they grew to be fingerlings, we let them go in Van Winkle Creek in hopes they'd return to make more salmon a few years down the road. Man, second grade kicked ass.

"Excuse me?"

I feel busted. The stern voice belongs to a short, stocky lady with red hair and crazy, red-framed glasses. She's got this bright orange teacher apron on. There are pens and string and tape hanging out of the apron all over the place. She looks like a clown . . . a clown you wouldn't wanna mess with if you knew what was good for you.

"Uh, I'm—Are you Mrs. Peña?"

"Yes. And you are?"

"Sam Gregory. This might sound like a weird question, but do you know a kid named Luis Cárdenas?"

"Are you a friend of his?"

"Yeah."

"*Interesting*," she says, playing like she's suspicious.

Her face bursts into a warm smile and she holds a hand out to shake. "Any friend of Luis is a friend of mine! I'm getting ready to leave, but tell me what you need, Sam."

We head into the room. There's clutter all over the place. It's all project stuff: halfway done balloon globes, maps, stories with pictures. Second grade, man. I tell ya. . . .

"How's Luis doing?" she asks as she puts lids on glue sticks. "He was supposed to be here a couple days ago. Tell him we missed him."

"Does he come here often?"

"Luis is one of my class helpers. He comes by Wednesdays. Last hour."

"Really?"

"He was in my second grade." She smiles and says, "Oooh, he was an angry little guy. He used to tell me his brother was going to beat me up if I gave him homework. Now he comes and helps me out with the new generation of angry little guys. I return the favor by chewing him out at report card time."

She starts putting chairs on desks, so I help.

"Those grades make me angry. I give him heck. He tells me I'm worse than his mom. Someday that kid is going to prove me right and make something of himself. Did Luis send you here? I'm always on the lookout for new volunteers."

"Actually, I'm looking for him. We worked really hard on this project for English class. Then he disappeared the day we were supposed to present it. He didn't call or anything. I came here to see if you knew where he was."

She offers me some licorice and says, "You know, every so often, he visits family in Mexico. His great-uncle. After what happened to his father, Luis wants to keep in touch with that side of the family. He never says anything about going. Then a couple weeks later, he's back."

"Maybe that's it. If you see him . . . can you thank him for me?"

"Thanks for skipping out on your project?"

"No. I dunno. Just tell him Sam says thanks."

"Will do. Don't worry, Sam. I'm sure he's out of town for a visit. Come back soon. You're always welcome here."

TEAM MEETING

BACK AT BOB'S, I tell the team Luis volunteers at Denny. He helps his second-grade teacher almost every week.

"You gotta be kidding me," Carlos says, disappointed.

Julisa smacks him in the arm. "It's the sweetest thing." She sounds sad when she says it.

"Mrs. Peña says he takes off outta the blue sometimes to visit family in Mexico."

"That's probably it," Rupe says.

"What if it isn't?" Julisa asks.

"He would have written it in the note he left me. He would have told Graves."

The three nod in agreement.

I'm rolling Tex Johnson's metal knob around in my hand. Carlos asks me what it is. I tell them the story of the barrel rolls.

"'Three sixty' turned into a theme for me and Luis as we practiced for the slam," I say. I tell them about us making complete fools of ourselves out on Pac Highway. "If I could go back to that moment, I'd haul my ass across the road and tackle that guy. Bear-hug 'im."

"You'll get your chance," Julisa says.

It's getting late. We review what we've done and make plans to go door-to-door in as much of the city as we can hit tomorrow.

Rupe says he can't come back tomorrow because he's got his meeting on Saturdays. And he's visiting with his dad, trying to work that whole thing out. But he'll be back on Sunday. Before he walks off for the bus, he says, "Sam, you haven't changed. You're the same go-getter you were back in Aberdeen."

Rupe has no idea.

He asks me if I could jam with him sometime. Says he has a bass.

I tell him I never learned.

"No sweat. I'll teach you," he says.

I tell him that'd be great.

I thank Carlos as he takes off.

"Not a thing," he says, heading into the dark.

It's just me and Julisa. "Thanks," I say.

"No big deal," she says.

"It's a big deal to me."

"He'll show up."

"You okay walking home?"

"Yeah, it's just a couple blocks. I'll see you tomorrow, Sam."

She only gets a few steps down the road. "Mendez?"

"Yeah?"

"Where'd you get that pencil pouch? It's a pretty nice one."

She smiles. "The drugstore."

"Seriously?"

"Yeah. It was two dollars, I think. I'll see you tomorrow, Sam."

"Good night."

"Good night."

She starts walking again.

"Mendez?"

"Yes?"

"You're all right."

"You're not so bad yourself, Gregory. Now, go home and get some sleep. It'll be another long day tomorrow."

We part for real.

I should head home but I feel the need to go update Mr. Graves. I want him to know an effort is being made. I could call, but I feel like telling him in person and seeing if maybe Quintel and Tre know anything.

So it's back to the Viking Glen.

MORE BREAD

ON THE WAY UP TO GRAVES'S APARTMENT, I see Tre and Quintel and tell them what Julisa, Carlos, Rupe, and I have been up to. They say that's great. Then we stand there for a minute without saying anything. Three guys thinking the worst. The only good thing about it is it's better to think crappy thoughts when you're thinking them with someone else.

"Son, get up here!" It's Graves shouting from his window.

He opens the door, and I tell him we got the search covered from head to toe. I tell him what Mrs. Peña said about Mexico. I tell him about the newspapers and the cops. I figure he's gonna give me a pat on the back.

Instead he says, "I need you to go to Highline Hospital and ask for a nurse. Name is Leyla Ibrahim. Somali woman. Great lady. She's a close friend of the family. She might know what's going on. I got her card." He digs through his ancient wallet and pulls it out. "Here. Go ask her where Luis is."

"All right, Mr. Graves."

I turn to go but he catches me by the arm again and says, "Wait, son." He goes to the kitchen and gets some zucchini bread. It takes him forever, but eventually he hands me a big huge square. I can feel the heat through the foil. "Take it to Leyla."

He hands me a smaller chunk wrapped in a paper towel. "One for the road," he says.

Tre and Quintel are waiting for me at the bottom of the stairs. I tell them what's going on. They say they'll keep checking in on Graves until they know everything is okay.

We pull out our phones and exchange numbers. They thank me. I thank them back.

LEYLA AND THE TRUTH ABOUT THE SCAR

AS THE BUS SLOWLY MAKES ITS WAY THROUGH A DOWNPOUR, I think about what I was doing on Friday night a month ago. By this time, in the early evening, I was buried under my covers, trying to sleep. Trying to block out life. Completely alone.

Now I'm working side-by-side with the go-to girl. And Carlos Díaz. Are you kidding me? And Rupe? My long-lost buddy. And now I'm crossing town looking for Leyla Ibrahim. Who the heck is Leyla Ibrahim? And whatever she tells me about Luis, I gotta go tell Graves and Tre and Quintel and Mrs. Peña and Cassidy. A month ago, I thought I hated Cassidy and I was scared of Luis. And I didn't really know the rest of them.

The bus stops in front of Highline Hospital. I hold my jacket up over my head to keep dry and make a run for it. The information booth is just inside the door. The old volunteer guy tells me Leyla works on third floor north. When I get up there, I ask the nurse for Leyla Ibrahim. She whips her chair back and shouts, "Leyla, you have a visitor!"

Leyla's young-looking. She wears a maroon headscarf, which frames her round, warm face. She smiles a serious smile and says, "How may I help you?"

"I'm Sam, a friend of Luis Cárdenas from Puget High School. He's been missing for a week, and Mr. Graves, this old guy—a friend of Luis and his mom—told me you might know what's going on."

"Yes, Sam, and please say hello to Mr. Graves for me when you see him. Come this way."

I follow her to an orange couch in the waiting room. Some little kids are on the floor wrestling and watching cartoons on the TV set. I try to block out their giggles.

Leyla's eyes look up into her head for a second. She's searching for words. This feels serious in a way I know I'm not ready for.

"Sam, how long have you known Luis?"

"A couple months. But I've only known him well for a few weeks. We were working together on this project at school."

"Luis and his mom are very close friends of mine. When Luis was younger, he was in the hospital for a long time. I saw his mother every day."

"Why was Luis in the hospital?"

"Have you ever noticed that Luis has a scar on his neck? He had a cancerous tumor removed when he was eight years old." She says all this stuff about how great Luis and his mom are. I only hear half of everything she says because I'm stuck back on the words *cancerous tumor*.

"Where is Luis? What's going on?"

"Last Thursday, Leticia said she found him in bed, home early from school. He was clutching his head. He told her the pain had been coming and going for a few weeks. He didn't want to go to the hospital and even made Leticia wait for him to finish some kind of project and promise him she'd drop it off at school in time. She brought him in for an MRI. They found that the cancer had returned and it had spread. They took him to Seattle, to Children's Hospital. That's where he is now."

"Is it okay for people to see him?"

"I'm not sure if they're accepting visitors. It's very serious, Luis's condition. You understand this, right?"

"I gotta go."

I realize I'm still holding the zucchini bread.

"Here. This is from Mr. Graves."

"Sam, you're a good friend," she calls as I bolt down the hall.

SPILLING MY GUTS

I'M SO PISSED AT MYSELF.

Pissed for having been angry with Luis. Pissed at myself for thinking the worst about him. I can't get the image of his scar out of my head. Not just the scar, but all the crap I imagined about it.

I hate myself for the time I spent thinking those things.

Mostly I'm upset that my first friend in a long time is so sick that he might die.

Couldn't he have warned me? Couldn't he have said, *Don't get too close and please don't care about me because I might not be around for long*?

And are we even friends? Really? Why should I feel all these things about someone I barely know? Should I even go to Children's Hospital? Would I just be in the way?

I decide I need to tell Luis thanks. I wanna let him know

that saying that poem in front of the class made things different for me. It made it better. And if I can't talk to him, I'll tell his mom.

I wait for the bus.

It takes forever.

I'm freezing. When you live around here, you know about the cold layer of wet that gets in beneath your clothes—beneath your skin—and wraps you in a chill that you can't get rid of because no matter where you go or how much clothing you put on, you're wet.

I finally get on the Metro. It takes me down Pac Highway. When I get close to the spot where Luis dropped me off that night, I swear I can see him up ahead, jumping up and down. Yelling at me with that smile. Making the circle like an idiot.

I make the circle in the steam on the bus window then pull the window down and squeeze through so I'm half hanging out of the bus. As we pass the spot, I wave at him and yell, "Three-sixty, Luis! Three-sixty!"

I climb back in and the driver asks me if I'm okay.

I tell him I feel a little better.

The bus drops me off.

I head down the hill and walk in the door, shaking, soaked from head to toe.

Ginny and Bill are freaked out. They wanna know what's going on.

Through chattering teeth, I tell them the whole story.

I come clean about the fact that I've been a complete slacker at school.

I tell them how Luis moved into my classes and that everyone, including me, was scared of him and thought he was a gangster. I tell them what Carlos said about Luis and his family. I tell them what Mr. McClean thought about Luis and about me.

I tell them how much I'd hated Cassidy for calling us *Luisandsam* and for getting after us all the time. I tell them about the slam poetry assignment and how it was Luis's idea to do it and about how hard he pushed me and about how hard we worked on it.

I tell them about the fight at school. How I assumed that Luis was a part of it and how that made me just as bad as everyone else. I tell them how mad I was at Luis when he didn't show up for the slam.

I tell them about the coffee and Luis's CD and about how it felt to hear my voice echoing off Ms. Cassidy's classroom walls. I tell them how I cried when it was over. I tell them how Cassidy cried too, and about how bad I wanted them and my mom to know what I'd done . . . and mostly how I wanted to tell Luis and to thank him.

I thank Ginny and Bill for the pizza and ice cream for my birthday.

I tell them how I've been trying to find Luis, searching with Julisa and Rupe and Carlos, and I tell them about what Mrs. Peña and Mr. Graves had to say. I tell them about the banana bread.

I tell them about Leyla and that she said Luis had to finish schoolwork before he'd let his mom take him to the hospital. I figured that was when Luis recorded the poem and wrote me the note. And I tell them that tomorrow I'm going to Children's Hospital to see him.

Bill leaves the room.

Ginny puts her hand on my shoulder. "Go *now*, Sam." She hustles into the kitchen.

Bill comes back with his car keys and his coat on. He holds a dry jacket by the shoulders for me to slip into. We head for the door and Ginny hollers for us to wait a second.

She comes out of the kitchen with a thermos of coffee, puts it in my hands and scoots us out the door.

YOU HAVE A CHOICE

Rubén, you know
  I gotta go
This pinche cancer
  has made it so.

I don't have the choice
  that you do
To stay here with Mom
  to stay true
To everything
  she's taught us
After all the love
  she's brought us

And abuelita
  who prays each night
That I'll stay well
  and you'll do right.

Hermano, you've got the choice
  that I don't

      TO LIVE

But the way you're headed
  you won't.

And it makes me furious
  that you don't see
All the greatness in you
  that you do in me

Rubén, you're worth quitting
  that pandilla crap
And living
  breaking free from the trap

That Papi couldn't

     Rest his soul...
     † RIP

Rubén, you know
  I gotta go
My white blood cells
  have made it so.

I hate what my body's
  doing to me
But I promise you one thing:
  MY MIND'S STILL FREE!

That's where your cells
  are multiplying,
Tiny gangstuhs in your skull
  are thriving

Invading every inch
  of your brain
Selling you
  on violence, revenge
    their insane games

Calling you homie
  familia, brother

Out one side their mouths
        and selling your life out
                through the other.

Rubén, mi hermano
  you've got the choice
    that I don't

        TO LIVE

But the way you're headed
  you won't.

I wish, for just one day
        I could give you my cancer
                and the priorities that come with it

So you can feel what I feel
        Want how I want
                Love how I love
                        See how I see

And this would all
  be as clear to you
    as it is to me

Te quiero mucho, Rubén.

—Luis Cárdenas

NO WORDS

BILL HITS THE GAS PEDAL HARD AND WE'RE OFF TO CHILDREN'S HOSPITAL.

I blast the heat. It doesn't help.

That layer of damp has taken hold and it isn't going anywhere.

We don't say a word the whole way. No sound but the pounding rain and the squeal of wipers bouncing back and forth.

MY FRIEND

WE ARRIVE AT CHILDREN'S HOSPITAL and follow the choo-choo train mural down a long hall to the elevator and up to the sixth floor, and we end up in a waiting room with puffy white cloth clouds billowing down from the ceiling.

Leyla said Luis was in room 634.

We get there, and the bed is empty.

No one's in the room.

A nurse comes by. I ask her about Luis, but she says she's just started her shift. I walk into room 635 and see a little girl, hooked up to all these tubes and monitors and stuff. She's sitting up, eating. Her mom is feeding her some orange Jell-O, and her dad is reading the newspaper.

I probably shouldn't bug them, but I can't help it. I wanna know what's going on. "Do you know anything about Luis, the kid who was in the next room?"

The parents' eyes get wide. They look at me like they wanna say something, but they just can't.

My grandpa puts his hand on my shoulder.

The little girl says, "Luis is up in heaven. He was my friend."

The mom has a tear running down her face. She doesn't wipe it away. Just lets it roll.

The dad hides behind his paper.

I look back at my grandpa and he's biting his lip.

The little girl closes her eyes.

I just wanna scream and break stuff, but I'm stuck frozen in rain-soaked clothes.

"Come on, Sam." My grandpa walks me down the hall with the puffy white clouds, down the elevator and past the stupid train mural, out to the car.

What do you do next?

We drive home.

Half an hour of windshield wipers back and forth.

Sweesh-sweet.

Sweesh-sweet.

Concentrate on the wipers.

Sweesh-sweet.

Sweesh-sweet.

I count each wiper squeak, hoping the numbers might fill all the space in my brain and keep me from thinking, keep me from feeling anything.

It doesn't work.

As we get out of the car, my grandpa puts his hand on my shoulder. "I'm sorry about your friend, Sam."

I can't say anything.

I go to bed and stare at the shadows. I listen to the rain pound the roof and I shake with the wet cold that won't leave me. I can't believe this is really happening. I slam my fist into the wall and cry until the tears don't come anymore.

MORNING

I KNOW I SHOULD GO SEE GRAVES.

But I can't.

I won't. There is no way I'm going to those apartments again.

Luis is dead.

I tried to make a friend. I tried and he's dead.

I go back and forth to his place, all over town looking for him. Worrying myself sick for days. And he doesn't bother to tell me where he is? Doesn't bother to mention the one little detail that he might die? Doesn't even have his mom call?

Is that what a *friend* would do?

I'm never going to Graves's place. I'm never going to school again. I'm never gonna get out of this bed.

I pull the covers over my head and close my eyes as tight as I can. I try to get to that place in my head where I don't care . . . where nothing matters.

I almost get there—

"HELLO, SAM!"

No! I'm sleeping!

"HELLO, SAM!"

Fucking bird.

"HELLO, SAM! HELLO, SAM!"

I press the ends of my tear-soaked pillow against my skull and into my ears as hard as I can.

Nothing will drown out the sound of that stupid parrot.

I try to pull myself up but moving my body is like hauling a laundry bag full of bricks. I fight against the weight and stand up.

"HELLO, SAM! HELLO, SAM! HELLO, SAM!"

I open my bedroom door. Gilbert is looking right at me.

"HELLO, SAM!"

I wanna hate him.

I wanna sleep.

I wanna give up on everything.

I wanna forget about Luis and forget about Graves and anyone else who's expecting anything from me.

"HELLO, SAM!"

But I can't.

I unlatch the door to the cage and reach my hand out for Gilbert.

Shhhh. It's okay. I take him to my chest and hold him there. I stroke his feathers. Feel his heart beating.

I like you, Gilbert.

I look up and see Ginny and Bill standing there. "Good morning, Sam."

"Hi."

We're all quiet together for a minute.

"I gotta get dressed and go see Mr. Graves."

Bill says, "Sam, I'm proud of you. You're my boy. And I'm damn proud." He and Ginny wrap their arms around me.

We don't say a word.

We just stand there, together, holding each other like we never have before. Then Bill says, "Now you go do what you have to do, Sam."

OUT TO SEA

I CALL JULISA. Give her the sad news. She sobs.

I tell her, "I don't know what to say."

"You don't have to say anything, Sam."

"I'm going over to Luis's."

"I'm coming too then."

"That's good, Julisa. Thank you."

I wrap myself tight in my jacket and start up the hill to the Viking Glen Apartments. I'm just a few steps up when I reach for my pocket. It's still in there. The letter to my mom.

I look back down the hill at the house.

I've always called it *my grandparents' house*, but right now I have this overwhelming feeling that I belong in that little rambler and that Ginny and Bill are all the family I need.

And that house is my home.

This place is my home.

I look down past it now. To Puget Sound. To Des Moines Marina. All the white boats moored up for the winter, bobbing in the midnight blue water.

I head down there.

I run.

I sprint to the marina and pull that letter out of my pocket.

I tear onto the dock—past a family packing up their sailboat, past a couple of old fishermen. I crunch that letter to my mom into a ball, sprint to the last board—

And I launch that letter.

I watch it fly . . . then drop into Puget Sound.

It pops up to the surface like a bobber.

The letter floats on waves, the tide pulling it farther and farther out.

And everything in it . . . away.

I take out my phone and hit the Contacts button. I punch in my grandparents' number and type the letters *h-o-m-e*.

LUIS'S STASH

I HEAD UP THE HILL.

Again.

I'm all sweaty from running and this shirt—the only dress shirt I got—is way too small. I know I look like crap.

I'm not ready to tell Graves.

I'm not ready to face up to the fact that Luis isn't coming back.

I knock on his door. Graves is cooking again. He has on a starched white shirt and a bright blue silk tie.

"Making some enchiladas for Leticia. She taught me, you know."

"You heard?"

"Yeah. Cryin' shame. I'll break down later. For now, we got to be strong for Leticia." He shakes his head. "I can't imagine the pain she's goin' through. To lose your husband so young, and then your son ... Sam, can you grab the plate of ham off the stove for me?"

"Yeah. Where should I put it?"

"We're taking it downstairs."

Now stuff starts coming up in my chest. My head tightens all the way around.

I'm going to see Leticia again.

We walk down the stairs, Mr. Graves taking one slow, careful step at a time. I watch, making sure he doesn't fall. We get down there and Graves tells me to knock. I knock and knock. Nobody answers.

I'm used to it.

"Maybe she's not here," I say.

"Open the door, son." It's unlocked. He walks in.

"Lunch, Leticia! Lunch patrol!"

"Graves, get in here!" she shouts.

"She's in his room," he says. "Come on."

We walk through the dining room. There are two empty root beer cans sitting on the table. Then down the hall. Luis's door is open. Leticia is sitting on the floor clenching tear-soaked tissues, looking like hell. There are a couple journals and all kinds of paper scattered around her.

She stands up holding a bunch of the papers in her hand.

"Look ... look!" Leticia has that crazy energy people get when they've been awake for way too long. She squeezes Graves about as tight as his little old man body can take.

Then she looks at me with a sad, intense smile. "Sam." Then her smile turns excited and she shows me the papers. "Did you know about this?"

I look at a page.

I grab more pages off the floor.

They're all poems typed on Luis's old typewriter. It seems like there are a hundred of them. "We wrote a poem for school, but I thought that was his first one. I had no idea—"

"Read this, Sam."

I start reading it silently.

"Out loud? Please?" She sits down on the floor and closes her eyes. She clenches her tissues in one hand and holds a stack of poems against her chest. I read to her and to Mr. Graves.

FLIGHT TO MONTEVIDEO

The crooked cracks in the pavement
A synthesized, memorized
Pattern in your mind
This commute to and from school
You know you could walk it blind

Step over that last crack
And it's five paces
To the 200th Street curb
And the blur and whir of cars turnin'
You count them like you did yesterday
And the day before

And you move on, block to block
Keep moving till you get to school
That's how you've worn such deep grooves
Into cement sidewalks
With the rubber soles of your shoes

It's Bob's 99 Cent Burgers on your left
Pepe's Used Tires on your right
In the King's Arms Motel
The Russian couple screams in mid-fight
Picking up the vicious argument
Where they left off last night

You've walked the banks of the Pac Highway River
Like a sandpiper-road-runner
Over and over
Till the view's a broken record

The thought's interrupted
As a jet plane takes off from Sea-Tac
And soars overhead
To Mozambique, New York, Tahiti,
Beijing, Colombia, Trinidad and Tobago.

Where the hell is that?

I don't know
But I wanna go.

The lights zap on in the Angle Lake Cycle Shop
And by the clock in your brain
They're running seconds late
Then—like every other day
The black cat you've named Cantinflas
Flies out the front door
Into the morning air
And you know by the afternoon
On your way home
You'll see him nesting there
Alone in the left front window
Watching you cross 204th
Again... just like the day before

Past the Self-Serve Car Wash
Where the crazy man sleeps
His sheets are cardboard
His pillow's an old lunch pail

You jump the puddle
Where the sidewalk's smashed in

And the water collects
Some days deep, some shallow
Some days there's no water at all
But the stain's still there
And you jump the mirage
Not noting the difference

There's Mike the locksmith
Opening up his Lock and Key shop
And the Midway Towing guy cranks his truck
And just like yesterday
You ask in your mind
        I wonder if the locksmith
        knows the tow truck guy?
Then you call yourself a dumbass
For wondering that again

The thought's interrupted
As a plane takes off and soars overhead
To Tel Aviv, Cuzco, Tokyo, Moscow
To Capetown, Taipei, Montevideo.

Where the hell is Montevideo?

I don't know
But I wanna go.

—Luis Cárdenas

SECRET POET

Tears are flowing down Leticia's cheeks.

"He was a poet. My son was a poet." She sounds amazed and surprised and sad all at the same time. "Why didn't he ever tell me?"

"It's kids, Leticia. At his age they aren't going to tell their mama a thing unless they got to. Isn't that right, Sam?"

"We wanna say stuff. But we can't."

"Can you read another one?"

"Sure."

"You have such a good voice, Sam."

There's a knock at the door. It's gotta be Julisa. This is all so heavy, I'm happy to go let her in. "Hey," I mumble.

"Hi, Sam." She gives me a tight hug. I introduce her to everyone. It's clear she's doing everything she can to hold it together.

She has some flowers in her hands. She gives them to Leticia and says, "Luis wrote this for me. I wanted to . . ."

She can't get any more words out so she shows Luis's mom the poem he had written for her and had gotten up the nerve to actually *give* her, which explains a lot about why she's here and why she was searching for Luis.

Leticia asks her to read the poem out loud.

I read another poem.

Graves reads one.

Leticia reads one. We keep on taking turns.

Leyla shows up with more food and she starts reading poems too.

As long as we're reading, it feels like Luis is talking. And if Luis is talking, he's still with us.

So we keep on reading.

TIME MACHINES

My mom takes in a fast shallow breath
Her eyes widen
And for an instant
The world stops

It happens when she sees Papi

Time machines transport her to "back then"
And in a split second
Back to now again

He's been around a lot lately

She sees Papi in the dinner plate she's washing
      white china from their wedding set
Sees him in the midnight blue Honda Prelude
      up on blocks on 208th Street
Sees him when the front door opens
      feels him in the cold wet gust before it
      closes

She feels him on her shoulder
      watching movies on the couch
         wrapped   in   his   tattered   Seahawks
         blanket
Sees him in old photos of the Kingdome
      And in that Cortez Kennedy jersey
         Our neighbor Mike wears

My mom hears Papi singing karaoke
      In a White Center bar

Even though it's really Van Morrison
        On the kitchen radio
                or Santana or Luther Vandross or
                U2...

She smells him when the grass is cut fresh
        When the Afatos are barbecuing pork
When the smoke from Graves's cigar
        Hangs in his apartment

Earlier today, I wished my mom
        good morning
She looked at me
        Looked into my eyes
                And she froze

She took in a fast, shallow breath
        Her eyes got wide
The world stopped

The time machine took her back
        And I felt closer to her
                And to my papi
And more sad
        Than I've felt
                In a long, long time

—Luis Cárdenas

MAKING ME BELIEVE

The same trembling hand
That reaches to shake mine
That grips mixing bowls
And wooden spoons
And extends
With offers of just-baked bread

That same ancient hand
Shook Dr. King's hand once

The brittle old legs
Fight to keep time
Behind the silver
Steel walker
Those wiry legs
Move his ancient body
To get the door
Each time I visit

Those legs once marched
In step with Cesar Chavez

His friend from the college
Shuttles him off
And those weak legs
March strong again
Against the war
For immigrants' rights
For the people of Darfur

The same voice
That says hello to me
And asks me if I'm hungry
And sings me Louis Armstrong
And tells me I can

That voice
Reminds anyone who can hear it
That there's no peace
Without justice
¡Si, se puede!
And bring 'em home now!

Mr. Graves's eyes
Look at me hard, serious
The look
Is reminding me
That I have a voice too

He makes me
Want to be better
He makes me
Want to change the world

Mr. Graves makes me
Believe I can

—Luis Cárdenas

Waking Me Up

Home from work
The sun rising
You touch my face

Luis, you sing
Buenos días mi amor

And you whisper the questions:

What beautiful thing will you see today?

What brilliant thing will you think today?

What amazing thing will you do today?

You ask without
Expecting an answer
You just
Plant the seed

No matter how
Angry I wake up
How grumpy
I might seem
The seed is there
And it's my choice
To grow it

It's my choice
To see and do and think
Amazing and beautiful things

Thank you for the mornings, Mama

—Luis Cárdenas

Next Poems:

i write 'em con ganas!

-The way abuelita prays, eyes closed and smiling

-All the stuff I wanted to say when Mr. Vaefale told us he had cancer

-Mom's time machines

-Sam in hood = turtle in shell

- Tre and Quintel, the gatekeepers of Viking Glen

- How bad I want to barrel roll a jet over Lake Washington

GOOD-BYE, MAN

EVERYONE'S AT THE WAKE. Cassidy, Carter, Leyla, Mr. Graves, Mrs. Peña, Quintel, Tre, Julisa, Carlos. There are family members. I meet Luis's grandma and his brother, Rubén.

McClean is there. He shakes my hand when I come in. Doesn't say anything. He just shakes my hand and pats my shoulder.

Leticia asks me to read one of Luis's poems for the service.

I'm shaking standing at the podium, looking out at his friends and family.

I close my eyes.

I'm in Luis's room again.

He's making the circle.

Telling me to read it like I mean it.

Dust to Dust

In church they say
That when a person dies
His soul goes to heaven
While down here
His empty body lies

And you should pray
So when it's all ended
It's a safe bet
You'll end up in heaven

That's cool
I'd like to make it there someday
But what if it
Doesn't work that way?

I'm a believer
In that you can trust
And I've read that line
"Ashes to ashes, dust to dust"

God created us
And nature, see?
So that line "dust to dust"
It speaks to me

I learned it in biology
That the stuff
God used to make us
It never dies
It just rearranges

So if heaven
Ain't in the puffy clouds
Or a kingdom in the sky
It's all right
'Cuz when I die
At the very worst
I'll live forever
Right here on earth

So when my ashes
Return to ashes
My dust to dust
My molecules-
All of Luis Cárdenas
Will still be here:

Feeding trees

Growing in plants

Flying in bees

Marching with ants

Climbing in vines

Falling in rain showers

Swimming through streams

Thriving in wildflowers

I'll be here

Growing

        Being
Giving

Always here with you
Always living

I don't have to have faith in it
It's what I know
That I'll stay right here
When it's my time to go

In God's heaven in nature
I fully trust
So when my
Ashes return to ashes
And my dust to dust
Don't worry

Just listen
                And watch
                        And feel

And be aware

And you'll know I'm there!

Amen.

—Luis Cárdenas

I GOT SOMETHING TO SAY

In line, headed to see Luis.

It's for real because this wake is open casket. People always say that like it's a creepy thing. I don't care. I never got to see Luis before he died and I wanna see him now.

My legs get heavier the closer I get. I wanna see him. But I know this will be the last time.

He's in a gray suit. He looks good but I hate that he smells like chemicals.

Standing there, I get this overwhelming need to touch Luis.

I have to touch him.

I look back and everyone in line is looking at the ground.

So I take both my hands and rest them on Luis's hands.

I close my eyes and see pictures of us laughing together. Luis laughing at me. Smirking at me. Us drinking stupid

root beer. Luis saying the poem like it was the most important thing.

I hold my hands on his for a long time.

Then I reach into my pocket and take out the reflection
Julisa gave us the day of the slam. Luis really liked her. He
needs something from her. He needs something from that
day. From our moment in the sun. I put the paper in his
jacket pocket.

I put Tex's knob in there too.

I turn to leave, then stop.

I got to say this out loud to make it real.

"Luis, thanks for being my friend."

EPILOGUE

It's been a couple years since we lost Luis.

I still get these waves of sadness that are strong enough to knock me down. It's hard to tell when they're gonna come. Sometimes the waves come when I'm really happy. It's like opening myself up to feeling great opens me up to feeling everything, including the ass-kicking pain of loss.

These days I spend a lot of time with people who make me happy. For a long time, it was just me and Ginny and Bill . . . and Gilbert. I love my grandparents, but we're a small family. Now it's different. Since Luis died, I'm surrounded by other great people. People I know because of him.

Like Mr. Graves. I check in on him every couple days. We talk and he teaches me how to make his famous bread and cinnamon rolls. And if I don't stop by for a few days, I get a call from Tre or Quintel asking me if I'm okay.

Leyla invites me over to spend time with her boys and Leticia. And she's got me volunteering at the hospital, saying hi to patients who don't get visitors. Sometimes Leticia comes and we talk to people together.

Ginny and Bill threw me a surprise birthday party this past year. They invited the whole gang—including Rupe and Dave—and a few friends I made at school.

Rupe is spending a lot of time with us. It's to the point where he's got some of his own stuff over here. Bill takes us fishing on weekends and Ginny mothers him like she mothers me. It's a little embarrassing, but he doesn't seem to mind. Dave drives all the way out from Aberdeen a couple times a month. The three of us get together in the garage and jam on some Nirvana tunes. Okay, they try to jam while waiting for my scrambling fingers to find the right chords.

We have yet to officially rock.

But rock we shall!

I've even started writing some. I work on the school newspaper with Julisa. We hang out and help each other on our stories. Mostly she helps me, but she's nice enough to pretend it's a two-way street. I've been writing poems and lyrics, too. Unfortunately, they're not on paper. They're in my head, waiting for me to get the nerve to write 'em down. I've got to soon because thanks to Leticia, Luis's typewriter is in my closet. I swear, every time I go in my room I can hear the thing nagging me to haul it out and get those keys popping. I can't put it off much longer.

So much has changed for me since I met Luis.

But one thing never will. It still rains in Des Moines. The world still turns dark and gray. But now when the view is a big, murky fuzz and I'm forced to turn inward, it's not a bad thing because my head's stuffed full of images that make me smile. Images of amazing people. Images of great experiences. And one image that I've been seeing a lot these days. It's a picture of a young poet and a crusty ol' test pilot laughing their asses off in the cockpit of a barrel-rolling heaven-bound jumbo jet.

Acknowledgments

This book came to life due to the combined efforts of these great folks.

Thank you to:

My family, Charlie, Maria and Laura Scott, and Maria Hernandez for their ongoing support and encouragement.

Aldo Velasco, for turning me into a writer.

Jennifer Christenson Wong and Kate Cassidy, for hosting the classroom poetry slams that inspired this story.

Kate Cassidy and Christopher Carter, for lending their names and voices.

Kirsten Heiken and Laura Lee-Walrond, for treating my shabby first drafts so seriously that I had to keep on writing.

Cristian and Moises Marquez, for sharing their thoughts on kids and gangs.

Carrie Stueck, for all the stories about her African Grey parrot.

Dave Couture, for the Nirvana inspiration.

Amy Amundson, Theresa Lucrisia-Bradley, Heidi Raykeil, Meg Richman, Wendy Rasmussen, and Cristian Uriostegui for their thoughtful feedback.

Donte Felder, for sharing his infectious enthusiasm for writing.

My mother-in-law Maria Flores, Kay Greenberg, and John Brockhaus, for using their students as *Jumped In* focus groups.

Authors Randy Powell and Anne Gonzalez, for much-needed encouragement and advice.

Chris Baker, John Brockhaus, Vince Delaney, and Molly Hall, for multiple deep reads and essential feedback that helped me prepare this book for submission.

Steven Chudney, for believing in *Jumped In,* for believing in my potential, for making rejections feel like part of a greater strategy, for keeping me focused on what's important.

Christy Ottaviano, for plucking *Jumped In* off the stack, for crossing out so many words that were getting in the way, for pushing me to fill in the holes, and for treating this project with such kindness and warmth.

My wife, Emma Flores-Scott. Emma, thank you for all the reads, for the ideas, for the time, for the sacrifices, and for humoring me by caring deeply about people who exist only on a page. Thanks for making me feel that the years of effort would add up to something in the end. I love you.

About the Author

Patrick Flores-Scott is a playwright, teacher, and occasional slam poet. He is a graduate of the University of Washington School of Drama and spent years creating plays with friends, most notably, *The True History of Coca-Cola in Mexico*. As a public-school reading specialist, Patrick has worked with students of all ages. His first novel was inspired by middle-school students who dared to share their hip-hop lyrics, a student who lost a long battle with cancer, and teachers who inspired kids to reveal their best selves through the art of slam poetry. They're all in the pages of *Jumped In*. Patrick lives in Seattle with his wife, Emma, and two little boys, Carlos and Diego.